Stephen Beveridge was born in Hackney, London, on 2 November 1954. He describes his own childhood as one of a rollercoaster ride. From being in care until he was fourteen, he eventually went on to have a career in the Royal Navy Submarine Service. His second job, after he left the Navy, was working as a practising field social worker. A job that left him with more questions than answers. He is now retired and lives with his family in the coastal town of Whitley Bay, England.

Alice

Stephen Beveridge

WHEN RIPPLES COLLIDE

Austin Macauley Publishers™
LONDON * CAMBRIDGE * NEW YORK * SHARJAH

Copyright © Stephen Beveridge 2024

The right of Stephen Beveridge to be identified as author of this work has been asserted by the author in accordance with sections 77 and 78 of the Copyright, Designs and Patents Act 1988.

All rights reserved. No part of this publication may be reproduced, stored in a retrieval system, or transmitted in any form or by any means, electronic, mechanical, photocopying, recording, or otherwise, without the prior permission of the publishers.

Any person who commits any unauthorised act in relation to this publication may be liable to criminal prosecution and civil claims for damages.

This is a work of fiction. Names, characters, businesses, places, events, locales, and incidents are either the products of the author's imagination or used in a fictitious manner. Any resemblance to actual persons, living or dead, or actual events is purely coincidental.

A CIP catalogue record for this title is available from the British Library.

ISBN 9781035843510 (Paperback)
ISBN 9781035843527 (Hardback)
ISBN 9781035843534 (ePub e-book)

www.austinmacauley.com

First Published 2024
Austin Macauley Publishers Ltd®
1 Canada Square
Canary Wharf
London
E14 5AA

To all the children in care that I have met.
You were my inspiration.

Table of Contents

Foreword	**11**
Part 1: The Beginning	**13**
Chapter I: So Begins a New Chapter	15
Chapter II: The Long First Day	27
Chapter III: A Chance to Meet Stig	42
Chapter IV: First Night Nerves! Maybe?	50
Chapter V: And Only Day Two	59
Chapter VI: The Manor Guesthouse	68
Chapter VII: Why Is Nothing Simple?	74
Chapter VIII: The Loving Spirits	84
Chapter IX: What Else Is There to Say?	96
Chapter X: Be Straight with Your Boss	108
Chapter XI: A Surprise for Claire!	116
Chapter XII: And it Only Gets Better	124
Chapter XIII: Thank Goodness for the Workers	134
Chapter XIV: Workers to the Rescue	146
Chapter XV: Two Dinners Are Better Than One!	158
Chapter XVI: The Sad Truth	169

Foreword

In an honest search for knowledge, you quite often have to abide by ignorance for an indefinite period.

Erwin Schrodinger, 1948

This book, story, or whatever you wish to call it, is full of factitious ideas. Ideas that may be construed in very different ways. A more enlightened reader will quickly gather that there is some authenticity behind this story. Unless, of course, you wish to abide by ignorance. That choice I'll leave up to you, reader.

It hopes to offer a fresh perspective to the accepted impressions regarding the lives of people who grew up in the English state child care system.

Presented within the specific context of the lives of three young women whose childhoods are drastically different. Claire being "blessed" with good luck within a respectable adopted family. And Evelyn and Fern simply through bad luck. Evelyn being placed into state care and Fern into relative care.

But ideas are funny old things and, when applied, they tend to create ripples across the still waters of life. These ripples eventually allow boundaries to be formed for the advantage of some and disadvantage of others. We all accept and sometimes too readily that these ripples, which are more often as not, created by the privileged in society, are not always generated by wisdom. Or so it would appear!

This book is created on behalf of the thousands of unlucky children touched by the inertia of the public child care system. Hopefully, it will allow some people from the care system, through the eyes and actions of Evelyn, Claire and Fern, a little taster of a more positive view of a care leaver's potential.

Perhaps, even another side to the constructed truth screened by governmental mandarins. I will leave it up to you, reader, to decide where the edge between fact and fiction rests for these three women from care.

Part 1
The Beginning

Chapter I
So Begins a New Chapter

There's a story behind everything…
but behind all your stories is always your mother's story…
Because hers is where yours begins…

Mitch Albom

Without any warning, the train came to an abrupt halt. Jostling even the most seasoned travellers, especially those who were already standing up and sorting out their luggage. For the young twenty-three-year-old Miss Evelyn Borowski, who was still sitting down by the way, this signalled the end of her long and anxious journey up to the North-east of England.

Without warning, the train doors suddenly slid open with the usual hiss and gusto of compressed air. Evie, as Evelyn was known affectionately to her nearest and dearest, stepped down cautiously from the train and onto the damp platform. In one hand, she gripped the old bright pink suitcase, that in all honesty had seen better days. The one lent to her by dearest old Lizzie. So how could she really refuse her?

Glancing up at the large clock on platform 12, she noticed that her train was spot on time. As announced by the guard when she boarded the train in Hull, the expected time of arrival being 14.12. And so, it was 14.12 precisely when she stepped off the train at Newcastle Central station.

The striking young woman slowly wormed her way along the platform until she reached the automatic barrier. She halted, reached for her 2nd class ticket from her bag and fed it into the slot provided. Only to have it immediately rejected by the unfeeling machine. A white, very plump platform assistant in her late thirties meandered towards her.

Well, at least that was the inscription engraved on the badge she was wearing. A badge of meaningless honour, so proudly pinned onto the right-hand lapel of her dark blue corporate coat.

On closer examination, Evelyn immediately noticed the heavy make-up covering the assistant's round chubby face; giving her that much sort after brittle corporate look. The attendant, whom looked completely bored with her job, stood with her bright red lip-sticked mouth unsmiling. Dark ringed heavily made-up eyes, full of emptiness, clearly waiting and praying like so many others on poor wages for her shift to end.

She snatched the ticket out of Evelyn's fingers and examined it closely as if her life depended upon it. After which she grudgingly opened the automatic barrier and helped the young woman through to the cold uninviting concourse.

Whilst re-adjusting her grip on the heavy suitcase and the small shoulder bag, Evelyn stood still for a moment instinctively looking around for the exit sign. At the same time, the young woman's crystal-clear blue eyes curiously examined the details of the old Victorian limestone railway station.

Evelyn, with her natural blond hair that was short, thick and tousled that suited her striking features, was constantly reminded how nice her hair was by her mother and Lizzie. Her mother had told her it was Aurelius in colour, and that was in fact Latin for the golden one.

Evelyn felt a little confused as she walked along the old concourse. She wondered why all these well-built modernised railway stations, for some unknown reason, allowed so much dampness to gather around the sad looking travellers. With all the large ornate cast iron pillars supporting the expensive thick sheets of reinforced plated glass; and yes, even this could not stop the predictable English weather invading the old Victorian platform.

The floor where she stood was damp and slippery, and in some places puddles had formed from the heavy rain which had fallen that very morning. She hoped and prayed that this was not some sort of warning sign against her forthcoming stay in this most Northerly provincial city in England.

Walking along the concourse, her mind spontaneously, and unconsciously, wandered back and forth to her favourite subject of the moment. And that was, 'Was she doing the right thing?' by accepting this six-month internship with a regional city rag! She had completed her degree in journalism and media studies in record time. And done well for herself she had to admit. Gaining a first against all odds.

Now what she needed was the experience of working in the real world of journalism and to get her foot onto the greasy unforgiving ladder of work. The real question for her was, 'Is this small city stuck on the northern edge of England really the place to do it?'

Her fellow students had plugged for London, Manchester, even New York, but she knew, given her background and her lack of resources, that these larger cities were well outside her realm. Well, at least for now, she thought...

Outside the station, the taxis pulled up fast and furiously through the rank. In her hand, she tightly gripped a crumpled piece of paper. Scribbled on it was the address Sam Lloyd from the Letting Agency had provided her. At this address, and in an area called Eaton, she had agreed to meet with him at 3.00 pm prompt.

Where, hopefully, he would show her around one of the more suitable properties that they had shortlisted together with herself and her sponsor over the telephone. A short-term furnished let with one other sitting tenant who, according to Sam, "...was a lovely gentle person with a great sense of humour."

When Evelyn revisited this biographical description of her possible flatmate, she felt a strange feeling surge through her body that nearly, but not quite, touched her soul. But more worryingly for Evie was the fact that it was presented to her by a third party and human trust issues still haunted her at times. Namely, a certain let's manager named Mr Sam Lloyd whom she had never met. Evie had learnt through the hard knocks of life; people don't often match up to your expectations.

So privately she expected to meet some unhinged lunatic who would constantly chatter and would leave the toilet lid up and the bathroom and kitchen dirty at all times.

"Where to, hinny?" The taxi driver asked in what she thought was an inappropriately loud voice, given that she was not even three feet away from him. Evelyn looked at the man and noticed what she believed to be some form a hearing aid around his ear lobe. So, she assumed he must be struggling to hear over the hustle and bustle of the taxi rank and the adjacent heavy street traffic.

Although over the next few days, the young woman quickly learnt how wrong she had been, and that it was actually a telephone earpiece he was wearing. She quickly learnt to understand that the loudness of the North-Easterners could surely only be down to their upbringing. An upbringing, she thought, that must have obviously included many generations of having to live within very noisy households.

Evelyn, ever the journalist and gatherer of clear facts, immediately noted how well the local young men had perfected their ability to project their voices over all other forms of noise around them. This was noticeably true on match days when the toon were playing at home.

The taxi driver examined the crumpled piece of paper clutched tightly in her fingers. Quickly, he recognised the address scribbled on it and they drove off without a word being spoken. The journey across the city took less than fifteen minutes which surprised Evelyn somewhat. It was nothing like a trip across Manchester or Glasgow which seemed to take forever, and often as not, driven at a snail's pace due to the inevitable traffic jams and bus lanes.

She paid the taxi driver seven quid and they parted company with a fleeting smile; but not before the young woman detected that she was expected to lift the heavy suit case out of the boot herself.

By now, it was just a few minutes after 3.00 in the afternoon. *Perfect*, she thought. The heavy showers that had hammered on the train windows that very morning had given way to a clear blue sky. As Evie waited on the pavement outside of the large Edwardian property she noticed that the house itself was situated adjacent to a well-established Victorian Park; that by the way, was guarded by an old tall and substantial iron fence that wormed its way around its whole boundary.

By the look of it, she guessed that the iron fences had recently been given a coat of black glossy paint that brought it back to life again. Strangely, this made Evie reassuringly happy inside. She liked time on her own to think and reflect whilst 'creating the column' as her old lecturer had put it. Although, at times, she did appreciate the company, but she could also become overwhelmed by too much intimacy.

At that very moment, a young man with a cheeky smile, thick brown hair and wearing a tight suit that needed taking up an inch and a half in the leg came towards her. "Hi, Miss Borowski, I'm Sam. I'm the lettings manager for the agents Shire and Moor. We spoke on the phone on a couple of occasions I believe."

"Oh, hello," Evelyn replied cordially, whilst at the same time shaking the young man's hand.

"And how was the train journey up here? First time in Newcastle, is it?" As Sam spoke, he seemed more interested in examining some paperwork he was shuffling around in his hands than to her reply.

"Journey was great and on time. And no, I came here once before on a shopping trip about two years ago with some other students. Stayed overnight then returned south. Never saw too much really except the inside of numerous cheap bars and restaurants."

Sam sensed a cautionary uncertainty in the young woman's voice about her move to Newcastle. The two people walked towards the large front door of the big property. Set into the door were two long beautifully articulated glass-stained panels, depicting scenes of times gone by on Tyneside. She immediately noticed that the property was really well maintained.

Evelyn had become an expert on flats and short-term lets, having lived in some hell holes after leaving the care system, compliment of social services, of course. She knew all the tricks that the estate agents pulled and was ready for them all. Sam opened the door, firstly by turning a brass Chubb key to open a strong looking mortise lock. This was followed by inserting a smaller-sized Yale key and twisting the barrel mechanism that withdrew the latch and allowed the solid door to open inwards.

At least good security, she thought. Evelyn looked the door up and down and was impressed by the lack of kick and punch marks in the paint and wood work. For Evelyn, this meant basically people used their keys to open the door. *Very civilised*, she thought. An encouraging life event that was quite missing in most places she had to endure after leaving the care system.

Sam and Evelyn moved into a large white-tiled hallway. For a second time that day, Evelyn noticed she received no help with her luggage. The only furniture on show was a small half-circled regency oak table set against the wall. On the opposite side of the hallway was an enormous white cupboard with many small doors to it, with individual locks on each one. She presumed these housed the many meters for the various flats.

On the occasional table mentioned before was a large stack of circulars and unopened mail which indicated to the young woman that either many people lived here or there was just a lot of junk mail pushed through the letter box. Instinctively, and given the geographical area, she thought it would be a bit of both.

"Follow me then…" instructed Sam. "The flat is on the top floor and up four flights of stairs." Sam moved towards the stairs and added cheekily, "It keeps you fit you know."

"Are there people living above the flat, Sam?" The young woman asked cautiously. She knew from personal experience how noisy some tenants can be who live above you, especially given some people's tastes in music sometimes.

"No, just a large empty loft space, which I must add is well insulated and boarded out." Sam paused for a moment, then added, "That is if you take it of course!" in a quizzical type of voice. He continued, "You can gain access to it through a hatch in the kitchen ceiling. There is a pull-down loft ladder fitted and it's all safe to use. Let's you stow your empty cases and things up there."

Evelyn thought to herself, *What I own, I can fit into one suitcase, so there won't be any need for storing things up there just yet.* She gave him an edgy, thin-lipped smile in return for this information.

"Will the other tenant be at home yet, Sam?"

"No, he doesn't finish work until about 5.30. But he knows I'm showing you around the flat. He works as a hairdresser."

"He!" Evelyn was a little surprised to find out she would be flat sharing with a bloke. She had taken it for granted that it would be a female share.

"Yes!" He said, and dryly continued, "On the phone, you indicated that you wouldn't mind sharing with either gender."

"I did?" By the quizzical look on Sam's face, it was evident that a frown had crossed the young woman's face. An uncomfortable moment passed between them before climbing up the stairs. Evelyn wisely left her large pink case in the entrance hall for the time being. She now recognised clearly that she was not going to receive any assistance with it from Mr Lloyd.

Sam opened the flat door with yet another Yale key from the large bunch held in his hands. Evelyn's first impression was wow! The decor was good and the furnishings were clean and modern. In fact, the best she had seen in a furnished flat for a long time. The large period regency sash windows allowed the afternoon summer sun to invade the large space. Throwing shafts of magical sunlight across the main room by the bucket full.

"This is the sitting room and communal area. The kitchen is through there." Evelyn's eyes followed Sam's pointing finger. "Your room is over there," he said as he moved towards a large wooden colonial door fitted with a fancy brass handle and a single ornate finger plate. Sam moved towards the door and pushed it open. Evelyn followed him quickly as though they were moving in unison.

She noticed that all the rooms were situated at the front of the large house and looked out over the main road. The park on the other side of this road was visible from all the bedrooms and the sitting room. She looked at the row of small terraced houses that were situated to the left-hand side of the large park. They were much smaller in size and probably just two up and two down affairs.

"Is it noisy around here, Sam? And be honest!"

"No, not really. It is a kind of lonely planet place for students in one sense, but most of the time you'll be here, the majority of them are away." He thought and added, "Exploring the planet and changing the world if you know what I mean." And then he continued "It's a short-term let you're wanting."

The young woman who had just finished three long tiring years of study felt there was oodles of sarcasm in his voice. Evelyn felt that Sam said all this with a quiet dislike of students which she never challenged, and in some cases, she could only actually identify with.

"Yes, between 6 and 12 months," she replied whilst examining the wardrobe space and chest of drawers. Then moving over towards the bed, she sat down and bounced on the edge of it. Whilst Evelyn wandered about the flat, the conversation for Sam moved effortlessly onto the night life the city had to offer. Stacks of music venues, local shops, bars and restaurants were only a short walk away and loads of buses that go to the toon centre pass the house.

Evelyn spoke in a whisper, "The town centre!"

Quickly, Sam corrected her, "The toon!" This took place on a number of occasions at the young woman's mention of the noun 'town'. Sam's corrective colloquialism went straight over Evelyn's head for the moment. Instead, preferring to concentrate on the matter in hand, finding somewhere to live.

Evelyn, who had planned to see two more flats that afternoon, felt instinctively drawn to the old Edwardian house, and the park was also a big draw for her. This will do nicely for the period she planned to stay.

"By the way, Miss Mortimer dropped in to see the flat last week." Sam replied.

Evelyn looked surprised when Sam said this and replied, "Louisa Mortimer?" Quickly, qualifying this, "You mean Louisa Mortimer from *The*

Paper." Evelyn quickly realised that she had not only asked the question but also answered it for herself.

"Yes, that one, your sponsor," Sam replied and continued. "She asked me everything about the flat. Was it secure? Are there any troublesome neighbours? Bin collection day! She went through everything with a fine tooth-comb. To be fair, she sounded more like your mother than an employer." At that moment, Sam wished he hadn't shared his thoughts of the woman.

Evelyn found it strange, as she had only met Louisa Mortimer once before, which was when she interviewed her in Hull about the internship. In truth, Ms Mortimer had also met Lizzie and the three discussed the internship in depth together. The budding journalist quickly recognised that Ms Louisa Mortimer was not a person to be messed with and apparently followed everything up personally.

So, she was not too surprised about this disclosure, and in all honesty, felt a little better inside for it. More secure in her choices…

"If it's any comfort, Ms Mortimer found the flat quite adequate and acceptable. Well, that's what she said to me. And believe me, I think she's the type of person to tell you exactly what she is thinking," Sam said smiling to himself whilst staring out of the window and seemingly talking more to himself in a low voice rather than to Evie.

Evelyn stood next to the large window and could see the neat picturesque park across the street. Tall hefty lime trees lined the perimeter of the large rolling grassed areas. To her amazement, a cafe was open in the middle of the park, next to a large stone water feature. She could make out that the water cascaded down the backs of lions and unicorns and then ran off into a large bricked pond.

Later on, she would learn that many children's pennies have been thrown into the water, and obviously the pennies were accompanied with a single wish for the future. Evelyn noticed that the chairs and tables were brightly painted and there were many mums and kids enjoying the summer togetherness after school had finished.

She felt relaxed with the notion that families used the park. In her hometown, it was quite a different story. In the majority of cases, the clientele of the city parks was generally to be avoided at all costs. Especially if you appreciate any notion of servility.

The young journalist moved away from the window and looked slowly around the flat one more time, calmly casting her eye over the paint work and decor. For Evie, and even more importantly, there was not a single ashtray to be seen and the floors were clean.

Evelyn announced suddenly, "Sam, this will be fine," slightly catching the young man off guard. "As you say, I'm only here for a limited period of time and the park opposite looks great. Will you inform the other tenant that I'm accepting the short-term lease; starting today, of course." Adding hastily, "So it won't be too much of a shock for him." Evie paused and then added, "So he doesn't come home and find a complete stranger living in the flat."

"Nae problem." Sam smiled, looked into his mobile and within seconds had sent a text to the other tenant.

"Done!" Said Sam.

They quickly signed the necessary lettings paperwork. All references needed had already been submitted. Miss Borowski handed the agent the necessary bond and, with it, two months' rent in advance. He quickly handed back the bond and said Ms Mortimer from *The Paper* had already paid it in advance. Both Evelyn and the agent were a little surprised by this.

It's not often that people are fighting to hand over money, thought Sam, but the deal was done, and the bond was handed back to Evelyn. Who it has to be said was a little confused about the money side of things, but she would sort it out tomorrow when she's joined *The Paper* properly.

For Sam, who flattered himself in the office that he was an excellent judge of character, was summing up Evelyn mentally. He only needed a single meeting with a possible tenant to understand if they were trouble or not. He felt Ms Borowski would offer him a hassle-free tenancy. Sam was proud of his intuitive character assessment skills.

These abilities, he felt, had assisted him in helping many gormless students, or alternatively helped him quickly recognise scally wags looking for a benefit drop; and more, had given him the necessary facial skill of ignoring professionals who felt the cooker needed a good clean, or whose beady eyes had found the one faded mark on the curtains.

Sam had seen them all come and go, but for some reason, he liked Evelyn from the word go. He felt there was a simple honesty surrounding her that Sam took an instant liking to.

The lettings manager left the building quickly. And it has to be said without offering Evelyn any form of assistance with her big bright pink suitcase. But slowly, and surely, Evelyn lifted the suitcase, a flight of stairs at a time, until she was finally back in the flat. In her bedroom, she slowly unpacked her belongings. Firstly, she removed the new continental quilt and sheets to make the bed with.

Next, she placed most of her clothes and things neatly and regimentally in the chest of drawers sitting against the magnolia painted wall. The wardrobe left of the sash window was a large pre-war type in polished teak with a long bevelled mirror in the middle of it. Her two precious dark suites, that Lizzie had helped her choose from charity shops, she hung up in the wardrobe, but not before smoothing them out with long sweeping movements of her hands.

For Evelyn, she felt she was caressing her future in the palms of her hands, mentally agreeing with herself that she would work and do whatever was needed to make this unique opportunity a success for her. She expected long hard days and she would give them unreservedly.

Moving towards the kitchen, she switched the kettle on and looked around the cabinets and fridge. Would whoever she was sharing with mind if she made herself a drink using their coffee and milk? That question was easily answered by the fact that there was no milk to be found. So, Evelyn decided she would not touch a thing until introductions were done and the boundaries set for flat sharing.

From experience Evelyn knew that things can become a little precious when sharing various items from fridges and cupboards, and she did not want to get off on the wrong footing. This was to be a new chapter in her life and she was determined to make the most of it.

From her hand luggage, she took out a buff A4 envelope. She removed the contents and read through the written offer again from Stein's publishing group, who owned the *Evening Gazette*. It was an evening paper run in tabloid format that had proudly reported on local issues and stories since 1885. Well, that was what it purported to be under the letter head.

The letter also provided the address of the main office on Saint Magdalene Street, NE1. Where she was to present herself at 9.00 the following morning 'sharp' as the letter instructed. She was to work alongside Ms Louisa Mortimer, who was the lead journalist for the entertainment section, covering theatre, cinema and local events.

Evelyn stood by one of the large regency sash windows with its twelve panes of glass. She stared out and studied the passing mothers and children, who were walking along the pavement opposite before they quietly slipped into the park. In her hand was a glass of water which she sipped as she reflected on her life. As long as she could remember, she had always been fascinated by cinema and theatre and the life it portrayed.

It was her mum who first got her interested; but with a lot of help from their good old neighbour, Lizzie. Together, they had spent many an evening watching old black and white silent movies on the dated VHS recorder. Dreaming together of all the characters she would one day play, or could be as her mum always sustained, when she grew up. They would laugh and cry for hours on end whilst sitting together under the old duvet on Friday nights.

At the same time, it did not go unnoticed by a very young perceptive girl, that her mother worked most nights until the early hours of the mornings, but Fridays had always been sacrosanct—their special time together.

Returning to the here and now, Evelyn recognised that this internship was a major opportunity for her and her dreams. With a half smile, she recalled how surprised the faculty staff and students were when the newspaper had chosen her above the others, and recalling the words '…they felt would be more suitable', although no one said as much to her face. Whatever that statement meant in academic terms; she fully understood what it meant in social status terms.

Not only the experience of working for an established paper but also reporting on what was her most favourite subject—the silver screen and events on the stage. And so much so, that she decided at the beginning of her studies that one day, she would be a film and TV critic. Her dream job; and now here she was. It may be the very bottom of the ladder but she was on it! Funny how things turn out, she thought…

That same evening, Evelyn walked out of the house on to Eaton Road. She crossed the busy street and entered the park for the first time. She sat alone at the cafe with the tables of many colours and watched with a little envy as the families played together. The play area was brimming with noisy, inquisitive and happy children running about at break neck-speeds.

She noted warmly the loving mums and dads, doting grandparents, uninterested brothers, interested sisters, whole families, including the many dogs all out together in the park; and all in perfect harmony with each other. A moment of togetherness that is priceless for memory making for all involved; but only if they knew it.

The still warm, late evening August sun gently settled on her face. At the same time, she ordered a bake potato, that in all honesty had seen better days, accompanied by a rather nice and ordinary cup of coffee she had to say. By now, Evelyn Borowski was feeling quite drained. It had been a long and tiring day and within an hour or so, she found herself back at the flat and looking forward to a good night's sleep.

Chapter II
The Long First Day

The question is not: 'To be, or not to be',
it is what we should be until we are not.

Soren Kierkergaard, c1900

It has to be said that the following morning, Evie awoke earlier than usual. She was never one for lying around in bed when in the land of the living; always feeling in her bones that something needed her attention. On reflection, she realised that she had had a poor night's sleep. Often drifting from a deep sleep to a more semi-conscious state where she found her mind playing out the next day down to the smallest detail.

Not because of the strange bed or new room. No nothing like that. Evelyn was used to sleeping in different places; it came with the turf of being a one-time care leaver. No! She had felt a strange obligation to wait up for her new 'flatmate' so she could introduce herself. Before falling asleep, she kept half an ear open, listening, half hoping, to hear the front door being opened, but it never did.

For some reason, she wanted to introduce herself and in return to meet him. Put a name to the face as they say. It was important to her that this living arrangement worked, and worked well. Memories of living with other young people from the care system seeped through her mind and opened those deep frightening wounds related to so many unhealthy memories of her young life.

She stared at herself in the mirror and shouted at her reflection, "Stop that! No time to be a victim today Evelyn…" She told herself to refocus, push the dark thoughts away from her past and concentrate on the world today. The one she had to navigate through to exist. The here and now…

She wandered out to the living room and quickly confirmed that her flatmate had not returned the previous night. Then moving to the kitchen, Evelyn had cereal and a cup of coffee, pleased with herself for having purchased the means of having breakfast the previous evening from a corner shop. As already acknowledged, and Evie being Evie, she would have felt a little anxious and uncomfortable using other people's personal belongings and food.

Her adolescent living experiences seeped through again. Especially the time when she had to reside with other care leavers after reaching sixteen. This period had taught her one thing. You should never touch anything belonging to others. If you did, you would be called out as a thief, a liar, or even worse for the simplest of things. It was central to the very nature of the care leavers' society.

She secretly thanked God. Adding quietly under her breath, if there is one that is, that that period of her life was now all in the past for her. It is all over. Evie's thinking was, if she never met anyone from the care system again, it would be too soon. A place full of raggies, tragic stories and unforgiving people, and that's just the workers she joked to herself!

As already stated, she would discuss living arrangements in detail with her new flatmate when she eventually catches up with him.

After a quick shower, she dressed. From her very limited wardrobe, she decided to wear a pair of black trousers and a white summer top that had a plain braided pattern around her neckline. Nothing too over the top, she thought. She pushed her feet firmly into the low flat slip-on charity shoeware. At that moment, she wished she had invested in a new pair for work. Well, unpaid work to be more precise.

The shoes were well worn in and had seen better days. Lizzie had been with her when she bought them from a charity shop in Hull and the old lady felt they had miles of ware left in them. Speaking out loudly to herself, "But at least they are comfortable, Lizzie."

At precisely 8.05 that very first morning, and as directed by Sam from Shire & More, she found herself waiting just past the park gates at the bus stop that he had pointed out so diligently the day before. Within minutes, a No 1 bus arrived. Ever cautious, Evie checked with the driver that the bus did indeed take her into the city centre and St Magdalene Street.

The driver assured her it did and watched as Evelyn counted out the exact number of coins needed for the fare, placing them into the cash dish in front of the ticket machine.

At this rate, Evie thought that her precious savings would soon run out. On the bright side, she was well aware that setting up somewhere new is always expensive to start with, or at least that is what she was hoping for. It was the one good thing she had learnt from constantly being re-housed by the local authority after leaving care—it gets a little cheaper with every move, that is if you look after your belongings.

The driver gave her a knowing look, as if reading her mind. "We do weekly tickets and monthly tickets which work out much cheaper than the single ones, lass."

"Thanks," was all Evie could muster.

"Give it a thought at least, lass," the driver suggested with a warm smile, whilst turning away from her and readying himself to drive off the bus. As a seasoned bus driver, he had seen so many people counting out their miserable livelihoods from their purses and wallets. Counting out one coin at a time like one precious moment of their life. Purely so that they can reach the well-oiled slave work stations situated all over the city. Or maybe he was just wrong, he thought.

Maybe he was actually offering them a journey of a life time so that they as free workers of the market forces could reach the great opportunities always available to them in the promised land. Journeys that would deliver them to that wonderful living wage and valued employment that is always waiting for them, or that's what most politicians would have you believe.

The bus trundled through the city traffic as best it could. Swinging from bus lane to car lane and back again every two minutes, or so it seemed. The drivers had resigned themselves to just follow the cryptic rules and the mysterious local council edict on bus lane use. None of the drivers really understood the logic behind the bus lane plan except it did seem to furnish the council with an unexpected windfall tax.

So, the buses just continue swapping lanes and swinging the passengers from side to side like a fairground ride.

Evelyn noticed a large gold hanging three-sided Art Deco clock on the outside wall of a big jewellery store positioned just above its fancy doorway. Its large black hands and Roman numerals indicated that it was just 8.25. A few weeks later, she would find out that this clock was known as *the* Northern Goldsmiths' Clock. She noticed that people were coming and going through the streets by now.

Many of whom she guessed would be on their way to work. Or maybe they had finished a rigorous night shift or an early morning cleaning job. One could never assume anything in this day and age.

The market holders were busy setting up their stalls in the part of the city that had been re-purposed and designated for pedestrians only. A flower-seller, she noticed, was arranging her green buckets on the pavement. The buckets bursting with brightly coloured flowers were placed in a way so as to maximise their natural beauty to her passing customers.

As the bus stood waiting for the lights to change from red to green, Evelyn became quite mesmerised by the many different colours and shapes of the beautiful flower heads. Flower heads that she thought were even more vibrant in the morning sunlight. And in return, Evie hoped that they were all silently gazing back at her with big loving smiles.

Smiles that were welcoming her to her first job in journalism and a new start in a new city. And in all honesty, and given the way she was feeling deep down inside, perhaps they were her only friends at that moment in time.

At the next stop, a large woman entered the bus, paid the driver and worked her way along the aisle and plonked herself down next to her. A funny thing was space, especially personal space, thought the young woman whose size 10 body was basically being consumed by her fellow passenger. Evie instinctively felt the woman's framework touch her left side in most places.

She examined the woman and in return, the large lady smiled and made a comment about the lovely weather they were having for the end of August. Or this was what Evelyn presumed she had said, having been able to pick out only a few of the words. Evie felt as if the woman could have been speaking a foreign language rather than English. She casually asked the lady, "How far is it to St Magdalene Street."

"Two more stops, Hinny," the woman pleasantly replied but at the same time, examined Evelyn's clothes as only a woman could.

Evelyn thought about the term 'Hinny' which she had heard numerous times in response to questions. She thought perhaps the origins were Norse, maybe Celtic, or even Anglo Saxon. Who knows, quickly realising she had more pressing things to think about given this was her first day at The Gazette.

Two more stops further on and Evelyn left the bus to be met by the familiar smell of a mixture of warm city air, overpriced coffee, food and bus fumes. Asking a passer-by directions, she soon found herself at the offices of the Newcastle Gazette, and all before 08.45, but in truth, still a little later than she had planned in her head. In the entrance hall of the large pre-war building, was a modern reception area with a desk intricately covered by an ephemeral Formica coloured facade.

On the front of the desk were the words 'EVENING GAZETTE' splashed across it in a deep red colour against a background of light blue. A well-dressed middle-aged woman sat behind the desk alongside a large man who was wearing some form of security uniform Evelyn guessed. Security for a newspaper firm, she thought. How real is that!

A nervous Ms Borowski handed the receptionist called Margaret her letter of introduction. The receptionist took the letter from her and, with a warm, fixed clinical smile, read it. Then staring down at her computer screen, the receptionist announced that she had to meet with the chief editor, a Mr Mortimer, at 9.00 sharp. Adding, "But before you can go anywhere, you need to get a badge."

"A badge," Evie said in a quiet voice.

"Yes, badge. We don't just let anyone wander around the building. If we did that, we would get every single lunatic and extremist running about the place raving about every conspiracy theory going."

"Do I get one here?" Evie replied. Margaret, or Maggie as she was known to the newspaper staff, never responded. But in what seemed just minutes, Evelyn was supporting a pass to all floors. By 8.55, and wearing a long lanyard with a pass attached with the words 'Evening Gazette' printed all around its length, she was ready for the day ahead, or at least that's what she kept telling herself.

Evelyn didn't much like the photo on her pass but in truth, photographs never showed the striking features of the young woman's face.

"You need to go to the eighth floor." Maggie, the receptionist, pointed towards the lift at the same time. "Then ask someone there where Mr Mortimer's office is." At that point, Evelyn could tell the woman had discharged her duties towards her and effortlessly moved on to her next task.

The brand-new shiny intern took the lift and walked out on the eighth floor with butterflies in her stomach. She was met by a bright large open planned area. The area itself was full of tidy looking desks with in-trays that were overflowing in a majority of cases. In front of Evelyn was a large desked area, strategically broken up by the many large glass partitions that were fitted from the floor to the ceiling. On each was emblazed in large old English and at an angle of forty-five degrees the words 'Newcastle Evening Gazette'. It certainly left one without any confusion of where one worked.

Evelyn stopped a passing man and asked "Could you tell me where Mr Mortimer's office is please."

"Sorry, and you are?" The man asked in what appeared an abrupt manner. No, to be honest, it was an abrupt manner. Unbeknown to Evelyn, it was the only manner he really knew.

"Ms Evelyn Borowski," she replied. Why she replied this way she did not fully understand. "I have an internship with *The Paper*. I was supposed to meet with a Senior Journalist Louisa Mortimer today."

The now past middle-age man, who was wearing a well-used cardigan, and carrying a bundle of newspapers, looked her up and down. He was old enough to be her dad and he smelled like an old ashtray. *Perhaps he's the cleaner or something?* She mused.

"Oh well…You need gold fish bowl number three, Ms Borowski." As the man replied, his arm and hand automatically pointed towards the office in the far corner at the other end of the long floor. Moving his arm back towards her with his straightened index finger, he was now pointing straight at her and made a circular gesture which meant nothing to Evie unless he was busy putting a spell on her. *Weirdo*, she thought.

After thanking him, she made her way to the identified office. Evie knocked on the closed door. "Come in and grab a seat." She walked in and introduced herself to Mr Mortimer. "Right," was his response.

"I mean hello, Miss Evelyn Borowski! Is that Slovenian?" The chief editor asked but before she could answer, he had moved on with the conversation.

"You're here to work on the Arts and Theatre desk with Louisa Mortimer, aren't you?"

Again, before she could answer, the conversation moved on at a pace which continued in this vein for nearly twenty minutes or so. In that short time, Evelyn had learnt that Louisa Mortimer, the senior journalist that she would be working under, had not shown up today. In fact, she was missing yesterday too.

Evie thought to herself, *God, how do you lose a reporter, a human being*? Well, in all fairness, she did not know Lou as well as the others, not yet at least.

"She interviewed me at uni. I've only met her once," the girl added apologetically and for a reason she could not explain to herself.

Mort looked up thoughtfully for a moment. "Do you know you're the first internship she has ever offered a placement to, and before you answer 'yes', she has interviewed dozens. And none of them came up to her scratch. But in you, she certainly saw something. I don't know what…"

Mort continued. "She's nowhere to be found at the moment but she will turn up; she always does. When you get your laptop, look at your electronic calendar. I know Lou started one for you. Lou has put in various meetings and engagements. I think tonight you are covering an independent film festival showing at the Old Art Deco Theatre and Cinema."

A surprised Evie replied, "Tonight!"

"Yes, tonight! You don't have a problem with that, do you?"

Mort's rhetorical sentence, and the way it was said, left her with no other conclusion but to say, "No, not at all." At the same time, she mustered a cheerful voice that projected a positive approach to life.

"Good." Then Mort continued, "Well, we have a desk for you in an office on the next floor down. Unfortunately, it's with the sports journalists." Mort wryly continued, "Sports journalists are a bunch of weirdos if you ask me but you'll get used to them. You'll soon realise that they have nothing to offer in life outside of sport.

"You'll be sharing an office with Mr Frank Cousins. He's been with The Gazette for over thirty years in total. An old fashion professional Hack who has covered horse racing nearly all of his reporting life; and totally reliable to hit the deadline every day for the press. Don't worry if he does not talk to you. In truth, he talks to no one unless cornered like a proverbial rat; and that includes using the phone too!"

The two people left the office and Evelyn followed Mort across the room. Evie felt that all the eyes of the staff were on her and Mort. The nickname apparently everyone calls him except when he's in a bad mood, and then it's just 'Chief'. Although wrong, she guessed that the reason why so much attention was being focused on her was that she was the new girl.

It was in fact that she would be the first intern. Something they all felt would never happen if Lou Mortimer had something to do with it! And then Ms Borowski suddenly appears leaving the staff in bewilderment.

They walked to the floor below via the stairwell. "It's quicker to use the stairs," Mort pointed out. Evelyn smiled and nodded in agreement. They entered floor seven through a single fire door at the bottom of a concrete flight of stairs, which shut automatically behind them.

"Whatever you do, don't wedge the doors open. Health and Safety boys will be after my guts. Nothing better to do I suppose," Mort said mockingly.

They entered together and she noticed that this floor's interior was not as modern or as organised as the eighth floor that she had just come from. It consisted of a square of offices situated around the perimeter of the floor, about ten she would say, and a large communal area took up the entire centre. Each separate office front was a half window at the top, a wooden panel at the bottom and a single door gave access to it.

The office Frank occupied was at the far end and had all the windows facing inwards blanked out with brown paper, so no one could look in and no one could look out. Evelyn was now nervous and was not sure that this was a good idea. Whilst they walked across the communal area, she couldn't help but notice that there were hundreds of pot plants everywhere.

Some over eight feet tall and the area resembled a small jungle. In between, an assortment of chairs and settees were strewn about the place. Evelyn noticed that the poor pot plants had not been cleaned and some looked very sorry for themselves. *What was this all about?* thought Evie to herself.

On reaching the door of Frank's office which she was to share, Mort walked straight in even though a notice on the door said 'Knock and Wait'. Evie could feel that Mr Mortimer would not be part of the occupier's games.

"Oh, come straight in, will you," Frank said in a patronising voice from behind his desk.

"Ok, Frank, calm down, I know you're miffed about Lou not being here," Mort said in a voice that reminded his long-time friend that he was still the chief editor at The Gazette and don't you forget it!

Inside the corner office, it was very bright. This was due to the number of windows it had been a corner office. In fact, Evie had to allow her eyes to adjust for a few seconds before she could see any detail. When she was acclimatised to the light, she saw Frank. *Oh no, not the old grumpy guy she had met upstairs, anybody but him*, she thought.

She looked out to the city skyline that, in the next few months or so, she would hopefully visit and learn more about, and tease out some great stories to share with the public at their dinner tables.

Mort opened the dialogue. "Frank, this is Evelyn and she's an intern who is going to be with us for about six months. It would make me very happy if you would try and get on with her." Frank recognised clearly that in Mort's voice the current situation was not up for negotiation.

Frank, who had continued to pound away on an old Olympic typewriter, stopped. Leaning back in his chair and with his arms behind his head and hands clasped together, spoke, "Welcome. You'll be glad to know this was the only desk available to you. So, in reality, you had no choice but to share with me. And in fact, it is the same for me and why you may ask yourself?"

Using all the best rhetorical sarcasm he could muster, continued, "All because Miss Louisa Mortimer has decided to take an early holiday or break, or disappear out of sight." Evelyn sensed that Frank and Mort had more to say on the subject of Louisa, and he was really miffed about something.

Frank continued to bash away at the keys of the typewriter. Mort gave Evelyn instructions to find Carol on the sixth floor. "She's the office manager and will sort you out with an IT account so you can access your emails and electronic calendar. She will also go through the usual joining things and organisational stuff. Fire alarms, canteen, security, and the like."

Mort looked at his watch and commented, "I've got somewhere else to be five minutes ago." He then left the office with Evie who, as instructed, went looking for Carol. "The office manager," she whispered to herself and wondered what Carol's job was in reality. In her short experience, most people had job titles that hid what they really did.

Later that same morning, and whilst Evelyn was being 'inducted' as it has become known in modern circles, Mort returned to Frank's office.

"Well, Frank, let me have it." Mort kicked-off the conversation with a knowing voice.

Frank looked up from his typewriter, "Have it. Have what?"

"You know, Frank. Where is Lou this time?" Mort stood by the window and gazed over the city with a furrowed brow and a worried expression on his face. At that moment, Frank realised that Mort was really worried about Lou's disappearance on this occasion. But Frank was never one for holding back.

"Well, she was going to be the girl's mentor if I heard everyone right. Mort, anyone with half a brain around here would have noticed that Lou never turned up again this morning." Wresting on the typewriter, he continued, "Leaving you well and truly in the muck with this half-witted girl in tow."

Mort spun on his feet towards Frank. "Frank, you can't speak that way, so choose your words wisely. The kid seems OK to me. I tested her with all the PC stuff and she appears to be down to earth and with a real good understanding of the role of a journalist. What I will say is this, Louisa certainly saw something in this kid or she wouldn't be here today."

Frank leant back in his chair and stared at the ceiling. "Well, Mort, I guess we'll have to cover for her again!" Mort glanced at Frank and smiled at the connotations of the use of 'we'. Frank continued, "She's let you down God knows how many times. Just because she's your daughter, Mort, doesn't mean she can get away with it forever."

"No, you're probably right, but look after the kid for a day or two, Frank; for me. But you know something else, Frank, I think Louisa knew more about the story she was working on. I felt that she was holding back on me for some reason. She had her teeth deep into something that both excited her as a journalist but also made her nervous, even a little fearful."

Mort glanced at Frank. "Just intuition. That thing you and I grew up with as reporters of times gone by."

Frank and Mort had worked together at The Gazette for many years and understood each other well. Mort was now the chief editor and Frank, at times, his unpaid assistant; although no one would say as much in public or the wrath of Frank would be upon them. In this time, they had formed a deep mutual respect for each other over the years.

Mort recognised that Frank was probably the best racing correspondent in the North of England. What he did not know about the racing fraternity was not worth knowing.

"Well, could you take her to lunch…"

Mort's voice tapered off with a laugh as Frank quickly shouted, "Not a chance. I'm paid to be a reporter, not an unpaid baby sitter."

Mort tilted his head to one side with a pleading look on his face. "Just for me, Frank. You're the only person I would ask, and moreover, you're the only person I trust to teach her the art of journalism. You taught Louisa and you know Louisa had that instinctive curiosity to smell out a good story. And Lou can certainly read past people's faces, so she must have seen something refreshingly different in this young woman, or she wouldn't be here."

Outside in the exotic jungle area, as Evelyn had already named it, she was returning from the potted history of the Evening Gazette given to her by Queen Carol of the sixth floor. In her hands, she had clutched to her chest a laptop, a mobile, and various bits of stationary, including three reporter's notebooks. Gifts of stationary do have a weird effect on most people, but none so more than Evie, it was like receiving hidden treasure.

The stories and articles she hoped to write in the coming months would be recorded meticulously in these wire ringed reporters note books. She arrived at the door of the office that she was sharing with Frank and looked at the notice on the door, 'Knock and wait'. Her blue eyes stared consciously at the sign on the door and under her breath, she repeated the immortal words of Shakespeare, "To be, or not to be that is the question?"

Adding herself, "And that is not the only question." By now, she realised that people sitting on the seats in the exotic jungle were watching her. One more look at the sign and she pressed down on the handle and the door opened and she entered 'her' shared office.

In the office, Frank and Mort were busy having a conversation. It came abruptly to a halt when Evelyn walked in. The silence between the three said it all. At this point, Evie, as did Frank, knew intuitively that they were stuck with each other. The relationship would unlikely be a harmonious one. But she was determined not to waste a precious chance like this internship on small pointless stuff.

Consequently, she decided just to get on with her task in hand. She had promised Lizzie the day before she left that she would focus on the big stuff in life. And just as her mother wanted her to be, something more than a victim of sad circumstances.

Evie broke the ice by adding to the conversation, "I didn't think I would have to knock to enter my shared office."

As the words came out, both Mort and Frank fell more silent, if that was possible.

Mort gave Evelyn a wry grin and walked out of the open door, but before closing it arranged to meet Evelyn again in his office at 3.00 sharp that afternoon. It was now 12.45.

In the meantime, Evelyn tried to log on to her laptop so she could access her email account. She glanced up at Frank who was still busy bashing away at the old typewriter for all it was worth, still wearing his old scruffy cardigan even in this heat. She just shook her head. To his left, pinned to the wall with brass drawing pins were old news cuttings which alluded to his column and the sport of kings, racing!

At this point, Evelyn realised that the laptop she had just been given was just about useless and still a black screen presented itself even after ten minutes. At the same time, both Evie and Frank looked up at each other. This was a defining moment for them both. Should they ignore each other for the rest of their time together or not?

"This laptop is broken," Evelyn remarked.

Frank looked at her and then at the laptop. "Really! Aren't they all if truth be known." Frank stood up, walked over to Evie's desk, stared down at what he felt was a tool of the devil, then walked back to his desk and sat down. He then picked up the old white baker light phone with its circular dialling feature.

He then put his fingers in the various holes to dial a four digit number, which was followed by a ringing sound. The call was answered promptly. "Is that the sewage works?" Frank asked.

"Yes, Frank, it is. And how are you today? We don't often get the pleasure of your humour down here," replied a member of the papers IT department.

"Enough pleasantries. Can you get one of your rat faced people to change a laptop? I have a girl in my office, not quite sure why, but you have given her an old laptop which is no use to her whatsoever. If you don't change it within fifteen minutes, I'll chuck it out of the window where it belongs."

"Ok, Frank, understood," came the reply.

"No, not OK; change it or out the window it will go." Frank replaced the phone in its cradle. Evelyn had never seen a telephone that worked like the one on Frank's desk. Although, she had seen them advertised in various retro magazines.

"I don't know what to say, Frank."

"Well, thanks would be a good start, Miss Borowski. Croatian, isn't it."

"No, Polish. And thanks again," was Evelyn's repeated response, although both their faces remained serious.

"Time for a spot of lunch, I think. Urgently need to meet a friendly snout."

With that, Frank put on an old worn green waxed jacket and flat cap. Opened a desk drawer, took out his reporter's notebook and two 2B pencils, then left the office.

Evelyn sat for a moment and wondered what had happened to her since leaving Hull yesterday. It was quite surreal. She pinched herself on the arm and left the office to explore the exotic jungle. There was a coffee machine which took most coins. Searching through her purple purse, she found some coins and fed them into the vending machine and purchased what was listed as white tea.

Two people sat on different settees and some distance away from each other. One, a spectacled woman of about forty, who was seriously concentrating on reading a book clasped in both hands, never stirred or spoke. Evelyn chose a vacant chair and plonked herself down. Whilst she sat there and drank the muck named tea, Evelyn reviewed her morning, and if the truth be known, at times she felt like bursting into tears; but crying was not Evelyn's game.

Not ever and for any reason. She knew from her experiences of being in care, it never achieved anything to show any form of weakness. Therefore, Evie had learnt to give up crying many years ago in the heartless system of care. She knew intuitively now was the time to show her true steel, guile and strength. Make Lizzie proud of her.

Now was not the time to show any weakness of character, especially in front of her new office friend, she thought, tongue in cheek. She was a little surprised about the laptop though.

She returned to the office and the clock said 1.15. On the desk was a brand-new laptop, with case and charger, and the phone had been changed and replaced by a brand-new one still in its box. Just then, the phone rang on her desk. At the same time, Frank walked into the office.

"Well, are you going to answer that thing?" Evelyn looked surprised at Frank.

She lifted the receiver to her ear and a voice asked if that was Evelyn. "Yes."

"It's Maggie on the desk. You have a visitor."

"I do."

"Yes, you do. Do you want to come down and collect her?"

"I suppose so." Frank gave her a hostile look. Evelyn quickly wished she had not responded in that way and felt a plain yes would have sufficed.

Frank looked at her and spoke, "I don't know who you are and, to be quite honest, I don't care but you are now from today a young new journalist for the Evening Gazette and that means something to me. So, act like one. I know it's not fair that Louisa has disappeared again but as a reporter, you must be ready for anything life throws at you. The narrative can change in a blink of an eye and you have to be ready for that.

"It will never inform you of what's going to happen today, tomorrow or in one minute, so be ready for anything, Miss Borowski. Go and ask questions. In fact, go and ask the right questions." At that point, he opened the door stood back and waived the young woman out of the office.

Evie was a little confused. She didn't really understand if Frank was being helpful or just highlighting her weaknesses. Let's remain positive and say a bit of both maybe, she concluded.

When she arrived in the lobby, a woman in her early-thirties stood wearing a well-tailored business suit. Not the sort you buy off the peg and definitely not from a charity shop.

Evelyn walked up to Maggie on reception. There was a silence between them until the receptionist looked up into Evie's round face. "What is it?"

"There's a woman here to see me."

Maggie looked at her with a look that stated the obvious. "There's only one woman here. Look over there." They exchanged looks and Maggie leant over the desk and whispered into Evie's ear, "Just to warn you, that woman and Ms Mortimer are apparently thick as thieves, or so they say. But I'm not so sure though." She then silently dismissed her again. Twice in one day, Evelyn thought.

The woman walked across the concourse followed by the noise of her heels clip clopping behind her. "Hello, darling, are you…Evelyn?" Both women exchanged glances trying to read each other. "I'm Rachael. I'm the operations manager at Art Deco Tyneside Theatre. Louisa asked me to contact you today and pass you the two tickets for tonight's opening of the Independent Northern Film Festival."

Rachael handed over two white thick envelopes, one with Ms Borowski on it and the other with Ms Mortimer's name penned on it.

"Thank you," Evelyn responded as she took the two invitations.

"Is Louisa in?" The woman inquired. At the same time observing Evie's shoes.

"No. She's been called away."

Rachael grinned. "Well, that's nothing new. I mean she has given us a lot of good coverage but she is prone to taking off on occasions without telling anyone."

Evelyn wondered why this woman was sharing so much information with her at their first meeting. Perhaps Maggie was right she was testing my loyalties to another. In fact, a stranger I had only met once and for no longer than maybe two hours. There was a short pause when both women looked at each other. Evelyn felt she wanted some response which she wasn't going to get.

"Well, I'll see you tonight then, Hinny, and it was so nice to meet you. And I'll try to find that missing boss of yours. Don't be late and don't queue with the punters, you're press!" She said laughing as she walked away.

She turned to walk to the lift with the two tickets in her hand and passed the help desk. She and Maggie caught each other's eyes. "Well done, young lady, remember if in doubt, say nought. Well, at least until you get the measure of them."

Maggie quietly uttered under her breath, "Hinny! Who does she think she is? She's from Leicester." This made Evie smile for the first time today.

On return to the office, a message was on her desk written on a yellow sticky note. Mort had to reschedule her meeting. It said, 'Go home and get sorted and ready for tonight and continue unpacking. You're staying whether you like it or not!'

Frank was typing away. It was just past 2.00 and she would have to be back for about 6.30 anyway. She looked at Frank who appeared to be dedicating his soul to the article, or perhaps sermon would be more apt, he was writing for tomorrow's issue.

She put on her coat and made ready to leave by putting the laptop in her desk drawer. The mobile she put in her bag as she would activate it later.

"See you tomorrow, Frank." He looked up and acknowledged her goodbye.

"Remember, Ms Borowski, that the arty crowd you'll meet tonight tend to speak a double language, one indecipherable, the other totally pretentious. Make sure you can spot the difference before you commit anything to writing."

Evelyn left the building and looked for the stop where she could catch the No 1 bus back to Eaton.

Chapter III
A Chance to Meet Stig

*Everyone you will ever meet
knows something you don't…*

Bill Nye

The red and grey No 1 bus delivered her safely back to the park gates. The large, deep red-bricked house gave the impression of shimmering in the heat of the hot afternoon sun. With the three keys she had been given by Sam, and with specific instructions, she opened the locks on the two doors separating her from the comfort and safety of the third floor flat.

Evelyn stepped gently through the last door and she immediately noticed a piece of luggage plonked in the centre of the room.

She was instantly met by a, "Hello…you must be the infamous Ms Borowski Sam texted me about. Is the name Czech?"

Taken back a little, Evelyn replied with a, "Hello, nice to meet you," and at the same time extended her right hand to greet her new flatmate, or so she presumed her flatmate, with a handshake.

They shook hands warmly. Stig was a giant of a man with a large, well-trimmed long pointed beard and short-cropped hair. Tattoos adorned his shoulder and lower neck area under the ears, which for some reason, was the current fashion. The girl couldn't make out the detail of the tattoo straightaway but it was very colourful and intricate.

A row of silver ear studs lined the outside of his left ear. Evie instantly felt that the hand shake was a warm and genuine one. Even though his hand was twice the size of hers and could have easily crushed hers, instead they softly and gently wrapped around each other's.

"Stig!" The girl said amusingly. "Is that Czech?"

"No. Long story short version, my parents were raving Catholics and it is too embarrassing to share anything else at the moment." He moved towards the kettle.

"Coffee, Ms Borowski?"

"Please call me Evie. It's what all my friends and family call me."

"Right then, Evie it is. Please to meet you, Evie. How did your first day go at *The Paper*? Had a woman from your work here last week; she was really something. Did she grill me! Is she your minder or something? But she certainly had your interest at heart."

Evelyn thought to herself that Lou Mortimer had never emailed or informed her.

"Louisa Mortimer, I suspect. I'm supposed to be working for her, with her, not quite sure what I'm doing actually, but apparently, she's disappeared somewhere and no one knows where. It's a mystery and certainly got people whispering at The Paper!"

Evie suddenly realised that she was talking to a complete stranger, whom she met only five minutes ago, in an open and unguarded way which was not like her at all. She had learnt well in the care system to guard oneself from any type of open discussion. At least until you are sure that they are either really friend or foe. This concealed approach still under pinned her ways to approaching others.

She knew from her past too well, the wrong word in the wrong ear and you could easily end up having to see some form of crack-pot therapist to cure your issues. Including a passing five minute unguarded conversation with a social worker. She had to do that twice in care, but with Stig, this oversized giant of a man, she felt strangely at ease; something she had not really encountered too often before, and this included her university crowd.

To be guarded was to be safe whilst in the toxic care system. And in all honesty, the university crowd were not so far behind in their toxicity of prejudices.

Stig handed her the mug of coffee. "Evie, the milk and sugar is over there by the fridge. Help yourself." On his large bearded face was an open and honest smile. "I've never known an Evelyn before, even at work."

"Sam said you are a hairdresser?" Evelyn replied.

"Yes, that's right, and before you say anything, I love my work. Done it for fifteen years now. Even own the shop you know." At that point, he lifted his mug and took a sip of coffee. "Up the West end of the city."

He caught Evie grinning. "I told you not to laugh! And what about your hair when was the last time you visited your hairdresser?"

"I've never been to a hairdresser. I go to the barbers. They cut it for me; it's cheaper."

Stig, whose face was a picture, could not help himself. "Never been to a hairdresser!" He said dragging out his words. "I just don't believe you. Well, that will all change, young lady."

"We'll see how things go," came her measured response.

For the next thirty minutes, they discussed the living arrangements, bills, and what were their likes and dislikes were. Both felt that it was best to get everything out on the table, so they don't have fall-outs and sulky days. Evie looked at the clock which was heading towards 4.00, and she reminded herself that she needed to get back into town for around 6.30.

"Sorry, I have to get ready to get back to work." Evie said suddenly, "I'm covering an independent film festival that starts tonight."

"They don't hang about getting their ounce of flesh out of you, do they." Stig replied.

Evie retorted, "I've had no brief but I have been handed these two tickets by a flaky woman called Rachael. She was not really clear what tonight was about. I think in all reality she was checking on her mate, Louisa. I think it's a series of short independently made films from around the world. Or that's what I've been told by Queen Carol of the sixth floor. Other than that, I know nothing."

"Queen Carol?"

"Yes, I assign everyone a title so that I can remember their characters and personalities. Queen Carol of HR who lives in a cave on the sixth floor and shares information like she is giving an automatic speech. Then there's Iron Margaret AKA Maggie on the front desk who appears as bit of a jobs worth but is a good person to keep in with. I think. Then there is Happy Frank who I share an office with. I haven't assigned him a title yet.

"I'm not sure who is really inside that personality he carries about with him like a heavy ball and chain wrapped around his neck. And there's Mort who is the chief editor. I'll stick with Chief Ed for him. He's a busy man and is the chief of the tribe of workers at The Gazette. He really was nice to me today in between his manic workload. Louisa is his daughter and has seemingly let him down on many occasions, but she's a first-class journalist.

"Or so I hear. Apparently, she really had her teeth into something, a story, but no one is sure what."

"It sounds a very interesting bunch of people you have to tame, Miss Borowski, and I totally understand why you want to be a journalist." Stig left the statement at that.

"Remember as the great American Bill Nye once said 'Everyone you will ever meet knows something you don't'. The skill is how you get it out of them. I should know, I'm a hairdresser and the secrets I know could fill your gossip columns ten times over." He nodded and winked.

At that moment, Stig's mobile rang which he answered immediately. On the other end was Rosemary all the way from Australia. Stig looked at Evie. "She's the person who had your room last." As Evie learnt later, she needed to return to Australia for personal reasons and had decided she was not coming back for a few years at least.

The voice on the mobile retorted, "Shut up, you overgrown Englishman." Followed by them both laughing. "No, really, I'm so sad you're not coming back," said Stig. "By the way, your room has now gone and it is occupied by Evie who works as a journalist for a paper. Very clever person; she is not like you Aussie birds."

"You cheeky bugger." The banter went on for a few minutes more. She introduced herself to Evie and hoped she would enjoy her time in Newcastle. She, apparently, had loved it. "Say what size are you, Evie?"

"Why? About a 10."

Rosemary carried on, "There's a suitcase of clothes I left behind so help yourself to anything you want."

"I couldn't."

"Why not? I told Stig to take them to the charity shops on the next road up."

Stig butted in, "And it would save me a job. And the embarrassment of explaining to the assistants what I'm doing with a load of woman's clothing." They all laughed together at Stig's predicament.

Evie thought for a moment. Well, it could certainly cut the middle man out as she would be most certainly visiting these charity shops in the next few months or so.

"OK then, but only if, and if, you're sure."

"I'm very sure," said the Australian voice from the other side of the world. "And look after that big oaf for me. He is as solid as a rock and my hair was never in better condition." She laughed.

"Then OK. And again, a big thank you from this side of the world. You don't know what it means to me."

"Hey, Stig, did you get that money I owed you? I transferred it last week."

"I may have but I've been away for the week. Amsterdam. It was great just the four lads having a good time and a laugh. Did I need a break as well."

After their goodbyes, Rosemary ended the call. Evie added, "I must get ready soon."

She stood up and went to her room where she took the mobile out of the box and started playing around with it. A very modern one, not like her old Nokia that was a bit of a joke at university. Just then, there was a knock on the door. "It's me, Stig."

Evie opened the door with the mobile in hand. Stig pushed into her room the large suitcase that once belonged to Rosemary. "Here you go."

Evie replied, "It's huge! Are you sure?"

"No, but Rosemary was quite sure and she meant a lot to me, she was a good friend and flat share." He looked at the suitcase. "Salt of the earth, even for a strait talking Aussie." He chuckled and at the same time took the mobile out of her hand. "You don't have a clue, do you. Leave it with me and you get ready." It was more of an instruction than a request.

The girl gave him a smiley type of thank you and he shut the door. From outside, he shouted, "Evie, I will never enter your room without knocking and you saying 'come in', so you can feel entirely safe." In an instant, a strange thought crossed her mind as she thought of Frank and the conceited sign on his office door. It made her re-think things a little, perhaps it wasn't so shallow after all in Frank's world!

She threw the suitcase onto her bed with both hands as it weighed a ton. Stood back a little and looked at it, then moved forward and slid both catches back, and a clicking sound could be heard, followed by the left and right clasps springing open simultaneously. She lifted the cloth lid until it eventually rested on the bed. It was a large, brand-new, top of the range suitcase crammed full of clothes and shoes.

She started to look through the piles of clothing. She could not believe her eyes; she had never seen such a wardrobe of clothes and shoes. Evie held a dress up against her body and she knew instinctively that it would fit perfectly. The shoes of various styles were well-known brands. She slipped her foot into one and like a soft glove, it made her foot warm and secure. Bending slightly, she looked down and examined her foot nesting in the beautiful strapless leather shoe.

At that moment, Evie sat down on the bed next to the suitcase as tears welled up into her eyes and leaked onto her perfectly shaped cheeks. Never had anyone shown so much unconditional kindness to her as she had received in the last twenty-four hours of her new life in Newcastle. She sat and sobbed to herself and wished that Lizzie was there with her to share this moment.

She would never have thought it possible to feel this way and so quickly. Up to now, she had to fight for every possession she had. Even at uni, the other students formed groups that reflected their own background and richness, that left Evie in a group of two—she and another guy who didn't seem to fit the model university student requirement.

Though, the upside of this was that Evelyn was allowed to get on with the course work without any distractions. There's always a positive side to life, she thought, wiping the tears away. But this level of kindness was too much for the young girl from care to process, in such a short period of time. She was just not used to it.

About an hour later, Evelyn left her room. She was much calmer and focused now and had pulled herself together after her warm shower.

Stig sat watching the large television in the sitting room adjacent to the kitchen area. He looked over at Evie and without a thought said, "You scrub up well, girl." Evie did not know if his comment was a compliment or that she looked scruffy when he met her. She let it go. She had worse comments aimed at her in the past and had learnt to ignore them. Intuitively, she took it as a compliment and smiled in response.

Stig leant forward and picked up the mobile from the coffee table and passed it to Evie. She sat next to him on the sofa as he explained how the keys and applications worked. Evie was a little surprised that she could read emails, look at the internet, and even keep notes on just one little machine.

"I've put you in the contact numbers as Evie. There you'll find your number if anyone asks for it. Also, I put mine, just in case you need something or get lost. Just ring me," he said moving his eyes back to the telly.

The time was now 5.30 and Evelyn felt she needed to think about getting to the Old Art Deco Theatre. She took it for granted it was in the town somewhere.

Stig moved towards the kitchen and switched on the kettle. "Another quick coffee, Evie?"

"No, thanks, I need to find out where the venue for tonight is."

Stig replied, "Don't worry, I know where it is and I'll drop you off. I need to go into town and meet up with a mate. Catch up on things you know."

"Why are you being so kind?" Straight away, she winced at this question and wished she had not asked it.

Stig looked at Evie a little surprised about her direct line of questioning and answered in the only way he knew by telling the truth. "It's what us kind Geordies do best, Evie. You need to get used to it." He recognised that this young girl was now on her own, been messed around at work all day and probably felt a little fragile; although she hid it well. He also guessed, and rightly, she'd had a bit of a tough life. All the same he had instantly taken to her.

By 5.45, Stig and Evie were sat in his old VW camper van and were heading towards the city centre. The traffic, as always, was heavy at this time of day as most people would be leaving work to travel home. She had never been in a camper van before and was surprised at how close she was to the window and road outside. Stig chatted away endlessly about the city and life in general.

Outside a coffee shop in the town centre, he stopped the VW camper affectionately named Daisy. He pointed across the road towards the theatre which was being used as the venue of the Annual Independent Film Festival. "Thanks, Stig," Evie said. She then got out of the VW and walked towards the coffee shop.

A few yards away, she turned and gave Stig a positive wave and a warm thank you type of smile. In return, he shouted in a loud Geordie voice, "Go get those stories, Evie girl!" She put her face down as many pedestrians were now looking at her, and Evie just shook her head in disbelief. It was nice to have what seemed a genuine friend to support you. And strangely only after knowing him for a few hours.

Perhaps it was being away from Hull but it was a little confusing, dealing with what appeared to be genuine people. What she could say with certainty was that she had so many acquaintances in her past but very few, if any, turned out to be real friends. For Evelyn, whose distrust of the world and people was well founded with a life in care. But this was about to change direction as good, honest people entered into her life.

Chapter IV
First Night Nerves! Maybe?

*Sadly, fear you cannot control,
but your courage you can…*

By clever people

Evelyn, who had only yesterday travelled from Hull to Newcastle, strangely found herself in a long queue that had formed quickly outside the Old Art Deco, as the place was colloquially called. At a guess, she thought that around about a hundred people or so stood in the line. The curtain was not due to rise until 7.30 and it was around 6.50 now.

A poster displayed, read that the Northern Film Society was scheduled to show about thirty independent movies in the next four days. Films of varying length and a range of contemporary issues from all over the world would be shown.

The first night was by invitation only and Evie was a little bit embarrassed, shall we say, to be standing in the queue. It had come as a surprise to her. She thanked Stig and wonderful Australian Rosemary under her breath, for all the help they had given her in such a short period of time. She grinned a little mischievously. Invited as well, who would have thought that, hey.

She could not wait to tell Lizzie every detail. Evie knew in her heart that Lizzie would be thrilled, and as was her habit she would clap her hands gently together over and over again like an excited child.

A few moments later, she heard the familiar clip clopping of shoes on the pavement from behind her. She turned and there was Rachael, hovering like a painted peacock.

"I told you to go to the front and show your press badge. You silly girl!" She said with such a loud patronising voice which drew the attention of the people queuing around her. Rachael grabbed hold of Evelyn's arm and basically dragged her to the front. Evelyn was a little more than embarrassed whilst passing the queue of film buffs. Rachael, in turn, showed no such reservations.

The two walked to the doors and a man opened them and spoke with a deep dramatic voice, "Good evening, Ms Cummins and one other." It all felt a bit over the top for Evelyn but within a whisper of a breath, she was inside the theatre and standing in the ornate art deco style foyer and box office area. Ms Cummins, and as quick as a flash, summoned a young woman over to her. Evelyn reckoned she must have been about the same age as herself, if not a little older.

Looking at Evelyn directly, but at the same time looking through her, as people who think they are better than you often do, she introduced the woman in front of them. "This is my assistant, Claire," Rachael said in a voice that the young reporter felt was unnecessarily demeaning her assistant. Adding quickly, "I feel that you will need all the help tonight you can get. Given that Louisa has done a disappearing act. Again. She will stay with you for the rest of the evening."

For some reason further snipped, "You'll most likely become big buddies as you have so much in common." *Talk about being judgmental*, Evelyn thought. She felt the hackles on the back of her neck rise but quickly controlled her temper, so she continued to present a calm exterior. Evelyn thought to herself, *Well, missy big pants, that's twice today you have dismissed me as a nothing.*

She looked directly at Rachael and thanked her for being so kind and sweet to her. Evie's voice was dripping in mockery. She had already awarded the piece of work in front of her two strikes, one for her obnoxious attitude and another for the unnecessary comments aimed towards herself and Claire. Three strikes and Ms Cummins would soon know what this young journalist was capable with her spiteful pencil.

Rachael had now turned her attention to others that were gathering in the foyer area. Many were friends and supporters of the independent theatre. Before she moved away, she turned back and asked Evelyn her name again. Evie looked straight back at her and said "Evelyn. Evelyn Borowski." Rachael moved off in the direction of the important friends of the theatre.

The two women wandered off together. "Shall I show you around the building, Evelyn?"

"That would be great. I would appreciate that, Claire. And thanks very much for looking after poor old useless me," Evelyn answered mockingly.

"And by the way you can call me Evie. All my friends and family call me Evie. But I feel Miss Rachael Cummins will just have to stick with Evelyn." They both smiled at each other knowingly.

Claire showed her around the various screening rooms. There were three in total. She added, "The documentary film you and Lou were planning to watch is on screen two. Show starts at around 7.30 when the directors, writer or producers. Or someone will present a brief description of what the short documentary is about."

As they stood on the gallery of the next floor up, Claire gave Evie a potted history of the Art Deco Theatre and Cinema. Apparently, it opened way back in 1911 when the electric theatre shows where just coming into their own, and the silent movies were placing a spell on their audiences. Plus, it always shown the news summaries for free.

Claire pointed out that there were no television sets in the first half of the 20th century and, apparently, the only way people could see the news about the first world war was in the news theatres like this one. There were no talking pictures either in those days. She drew Evie's attention to the building itself and the many original architectural features that remained to this day.

Claire said in a melancholy voice, "Sadly, a bomb in 1943 had destroyed some murals commissioned by the owners. A local artist called Bessie McCarron had decorated both the restaurant and the adjacent smoking-room walls by painting various Greco Romano frescoes. One, apparently, depicted the Canterbury Tales. But they were all destroyed in the fire after the bomb had hit.

"I find it so sad when something so uniquely created by art or literature is destroyed for whatever reason. But especially war." Evie just nodded in agreement.

At last, they ended up at the top of the building where there was food and drinks laid out on the bare wooden tables. The women helped themselves and chatted about their love of the silent movies and discussed the great actresses of the past. Evie leant over and whispered in Claire's ear, "How do you put up with that smug attitude of Rachael's?" Both girls laughed.

"I do what you do," Claire whispered back. "I play her. In a few months' time, the board here will know exactly who does what. I promise you that." The girls clinked glasses and again laughed knowingly and cheekily. "Moreover, I love working here, and that woman is not going to prevent me from working where I most want to be, deep in the history of theatre, art and cinema." There was strength in the woman's voice that Evie could connect with.

Claire directed Evie's eyes to the floor of the area where they both stood. She drew her attention to the re-exposed exquisite Italian glass mosaic floor that dated back to around 1936. Over their heads was a large silver mirrored ballroom globe slowly and silently spinning around, throwing off speckled shapes of bright white light across the coloured Italian glass floor with its complex pattern that seemed to twinkle back at the two women.

What may be surprising to others was that these two young people were quite capable of appreciating the Italian glass floors, that combined together, provided both utility and aesthetics, which had only been re-exposed for a couple of years. Apparently, it had been over laid by modern floor tiles in the 90s. In an attempt, it is said, to radically modernise the theatre.

And somehow make it more fashionable and hopefully attract the new middle class fine art student types flooding the local universities at the time, and hopefully bring them through the doors. Sadly, this never worked and again the theatre went into decline for a short while. "Thank goodness for common sense," Evie remarked and again chinked Claire's glass of orange juice. She added, "Common sense is now our responsibility."

Again, they chinked glasses. "To common sense!" They both said in unison.

"By the way, Evie, Louisa Mortimer, who you'll be working with, is as sharp as a tack. And in all honesty, only puts up with Rachael to hear all the gossip. She just feeds her vanity to get insider information."

Leaning over to Evie, Claire asked, "What happened to her anyway?"

"No one seems to know but I do feel that Mort, Chief Ed and father of the errant reporter, is really worried. Hasn't said as much but it is in his eyes and face."

"A face reader, hey?" Claire asked.

"Where I'm from, it's best you read the faces of the others before you get cornered by the rats that circle around you."

"Like that, is it?" Claire's head tilted slightly to one side in an acknowledgement of the caustic indictment of humanity Evie presented.

"Very much so. I'm afraid to say," responded Evie.

With that, the bell sounded announcing that the show will start in five minutes and can people start to take their seats. Claire and Evie moved into the auditorium and took their allocated seats. As Louisa was still a no show, Claire had plonked herself down in a seat at the front next to Evie. They were now quiet and the journalist took her reporter's notebook and 2B pencil out of her bag, adjusted herself in the seat and made ready for the film and presentation.

Claire leant over the arm of the chair and quietly pointed out that this row was potentially full of journalists and hacks from various periodicals. She looked along the row and people were returning her glances and then looking away. "They all want to know where Lou is and what the score is. They'll zoom into you later; you can be assured of that. My advice, tell them nothing."

"That won't be hard, will it? Because I don't know anything."

The lights started to dim. On stage, two spotlights came on and three people walked on to the stage. One a man and two elderly ladies dressed in a fashion that was best suited for a Miss Marple movie. The man went to the mike and opened the session by introducing the two ladies who had been the benefactors behind the short documentary called 'The Devil's Church'.

"It is a story of how the church in the past have corroborated and helped various right-wing organisations." Just as he was about to continue his opening address, the lights came on again, and two men walked blatantly onto the stage, and stood in front of the man with the mike. One a priest and the other a well-dressed and groomed man in a dark grey suit. They moved quickly to the speakers followed by a very flustered and startled Rachael.

A conversation took place between the parties on the stage. You could not make out the words being said but all parties were furious with each other and an argument broke out. Rachael stood with her mouth gaping open and was lost for words to say. Claire thought Ms Racheal Cummins was only good with words when it was a one-way conversation.

Instinctively, Claire jumped up and then quickly moved the ten paces towards the stairs to the stage. She quickly reached the group and strongly insisted that they all move away from the stage and maybe continue their discussion in one of the upper floor offices, so that whatever they needed to say was said in private. The tall and slim man in the expensive suit handed Claire an envelope that she instinctively took.

He told Claire that she and the theatre had been served with an injunction, and that the documentary planned to be shown could not be disclosed until a court of law had overturned the injunction.

Claire as quick as a flash passed it to Rachael. "I think this is your pay grade." Claire then ruthlessly ushered them off the stage. At that moment, all the lights came back on to find Rachael standing rooted to a spot with the envelope in her hand and totally lost what to do. Apparently, there was no policy and procedure for this uproar.

There was now a loud buzzing coming from the audience, people basically asking in raised voices what was going on. "What do you know?" Many made a bee-line towards poor Evelyn, expecting her to have answers when in fact she was as much in the dark as to what was going on as they were.

"Hello, I'm Mike from independent cinema magazine."

"Hello, I'm Sarah North-East monthly, how nice to meet you. I never caught your name."

"I never gave it!" Evelyn coldly replied. A haggle of journalists can be like a shoal of feeding piranhas when they smell meat.

"Excuse me, I need to go to the loo." With that excuse, Evelyn moved away from the two hundred or so people in the auditorium. Some, a small group, were shouting something about freedom of speech and how the churches were worse than politicians.

On the way to the loo, Evie bumped into Claire on the stairs. "Hi. I was just about to fetch you. In fact, they asked me to get you. Rachael's in a right tizzy and putting on her coat! They are talking about some documentary that cannot be shown and apparently, Lou was about to print an article in the paper tomorrow about it. According to the two ladies who were on the stage, she had already written it and it was ready for publishing."

Evelyn, ushered by Claire, entered the private space. All hell was breaking out between the priest, the man in the expensive suit and the two old ladies dressed like Miss Marple figures, with matching coats and costumes. The priest, who may not have been more than thirty or so, was sweating liberally from his forehead. He made threats as to what would happen if these treacherous lies were ever to be broadcasted to the public.

The man with him tried to calm him down and reason with them all. Rachael was so out of her depth that even a shed full of policies and procedures could not have helped her at that moment. Claire moved towards the group in the private office and introduced Evelyn as a journalist from the Evening Gazette. At that moment she was not sure if she was a journalist for the Evening Gazette or a witness to an all-out war of some kind.

The five people looked towards Evelyn. The priest introduced himself as Father O'Keith. At this point, the taller of the two women retorted, "He is certainly not a father! We know the names of all the fathers."

The other woman interrupted, "Neither are the bullying nuns really anyone's sisters we'll have you know." This physically riled the priest.

"What has the paper to say for itself!" The priest asked.

As quick as a flash, Evie replied, "Nothing, how can we? None of us have seen the documentary that was supposed to have been shown about ten minutes ago. And given someone has served an injunction, I would suggest that I won't be seeing it tonight either. If ever!" The young journalist spoke in a clear and measured voice.

"Well, make sure you don't," commanded the priest. "If you do, this place will be taken down brick by brick and dragged through the courts for its lies and treachery it was about to show."

Evelyn thought that the priest was about to have a heart attack. He kept grabbing at his dog collar and his face was nearly purple.

"We're leaving," said the taller of the two ladies, "but it is not finished by a long chalk." She continued, "The church that always hides behind a dark cloak of righteousness. You, Mr O'Keith," the taller woman pointing angrily at the priest, "know nothing but what you are told and want to believe. But we were there. Our families were there and the truth will come out."

It was obvious that the priest was livid that the woman had addressed him as Mr O'Keith, and replied, "Father O'Keith if you would, please."

"No, I would not please you or any other member of the Devil's brigade. This has not ended because of that legal scrap of paper you managed to whip up from some legal friend of the devil's church."

Enid looked at the taller woman appealingly, "Edith, let's go." Both women left with the younger man.

Evelyn left the office quickly followed by Claire. "God, what just happened in there?" Claire asked.

Evelyn replied, "I don't know but I will find out. But where the bloody hell is Lou Mortimer when you need her?"

Evie's quick thinking saw her tearing down the stairs and soon she was standing next to the two ladies. Both stared at Evie with a look of disappointment and regret on their faces.

"Ms Mortimer was supposed to meet with us this afternoon but she never turned up!"

Evie replied, "I know. Everyone is looking for her and her parents seem really worried about her. Well, I think so anyhow. But you must understand that I only started at the paper this morning. You can't believe what sort of day this has turned out to be."

Ms Taylor pondered over the girl in front of her calmly and suspiciously before replying, "I think it's been a bad day for many of us, my dear. Many more people than you can even envisage actually." Squinting at her, Edith then asked "What's your name again?"

"Evelyn Borowski, Ma'am. I'm an intern supposedly working for Lou. I've only actually met her once. That was when she interviewed me."

The two outwardly prudish women moved Evelyn away and out of the hearing of the general public. Just then, a journalist who tried to introduce himself earlier, came over and stood close to the three women. "Hello, what's going on here then?" He said with what was clearly an artificial smile.

Evelyn spun around to face him full on. "Go away! You are not invited to this conversation." With that, the taller lady at the same time turned towards the man and waved him away. The reporter left the three women in the lobby but from the expression on his face, he was not a happy bunny in any sense of the word. As Evie would later find out.

The taller sister spoke, "Look, this is not the place or time to discuss the documentary we had made and the work we had done with Ms Mortimer. If you look in your calendar, you will notice that you and Lou are due to meet with us on Saturday morning in Ireland. All travel arrangements have been made for tomorrow night on a flight from Newcastle to Belfast. Make sure you read your emails, Ms Borowski. We'll talk when you come to Northern Ireland at the weekend."

Evie's head now spinning, replied without thinking, "Ireland, what are you on about?"

Enid passed her a card, and then the taller lady instructed, "Ring me tomorrow and confirm your arrival time. I'm sure you'll know more by then." The woman turned her back one more time and continued. "Louisa Mortimer was an excellent journalist and reporter and she picked you, Ms Borowski, for a reason. But I'm not quite sure why yet." Her words hung in the air for a few moments.

Then raising her eyebrows and in a stern school ma'am fashion, she turned away with Enid, her twin sister by birth. They both left the theatre foyer and moved into the dark city night. A well-groomed, tall stocky man, in a neat black suit, was waiting outside the theatre for them. He moved closer to them and guided them to the waiting car. Always walking behind the two of them, in what can only be described as a protective way.

At the very same moment they left the theatre, Claire caught up with Evelyn again in the foyer. On the stairs behind her were the priest and well-dressed gentleman who were also making their way towards the exit doors with great haste.

Claire and Evie glanced at each other and both agreed that it was a seriously mad evening so far. "Are they always like this?" Evelyn asked. The two young women, now joined at the hip as insisted by the delectable Rachael, moved onto another showing. A documentary styled film about life for a woman inside the Islamic State.

Following this showing, Evie pushed to leave as she wanted to get back to the flat and write up some significant notes on the events which had just taken place before they became distorted or vague in the memory of time and sleep. In fact, it was a habit of Evelyn to write up accurate notes as soon as possible. It was one of her traits that had got her noticed at university—always going the extra mile.

With this, both girls slipped out of the theatre. Claire gave Evie a lift home in her car as it was on her way to the coast, where she still lived with her parents. Claire stopped outside the large house on Eaton Road.

"Will you get into trouble for leaving early?" Evelyn asked pointedly.

"No. I'm like you, Evie, an unpaid intern, a no one. Rachael only notices me when she is looking for a coffee." With this, they both wished each other good night. Claire said she would phone her in the morning for a catch-up.

Then Evie waved good night as Claire pulled off.

Chapter V
And Only Day Two

*We are buried beneath the weight of information,
which is being confused with knowledge.*

Tom Waite

Day two and our Evie was back on the No 1 bus. The same driver was on the bus as yesterday. Again, she bought only a single ticket instead of a return. "Next week perhaps? A weekly ticket." In response, she grinned at the driver, who gave her a cheerful smile in return saying, "It's much cheaper, missy, you know."

Her eyes followed the outside world as the journey to work took place. She was happy with the three pages of notes she had managed to jot down before going to sleep. She had not seen Stig, but thought he must have gone to bed early. The Northern Guild of Goldsmiths clock was reporting the time as 08.18, a little earlier than yesterday she noted.

By 8.45, she was at her desk. No sooner had she sat down than the phone rang. Unassumingly, she answered as she did not really understand her role at The Gazette yet. "Is that you, Evelyn?"

"Yes," she replied.

"It's Mr Mortimer, can you come up to my office on the eighth…"

"Of course. I'm on my way." She left the office and then turned back and picked up her notebook with the recordings of last night's shenanigans. Within minutes, she was knocking on his door in goldfish bowl number 3, as Frank comically put it.

An order followed, "Come in take a seat."

In the office were Mort and Frank, both who were drinking coffee that had been bought before they arrived at work. "Sorry, can't offer you anything, Ms Borowski," said Mort.

Mort relayed the conversation he had on the phone last night with Doug Collingwood, the Chair of the Board of Trustees of the Art Deco Theatre, and a good friend. He shared what had happened. Relaying that a commotion or protest had taken place the evening before, just prior to the showing of a short independent film called 'The Devil's Children'. He went on to say, "Doug wanted to pass on his thanks to you for keeping cool and helping sort out the chaos."

Mort continued, "These outbursts often happened at these independent film festivals, especially when people are showing fringe films. It comes with the turf when screening documentaries about genocides or the discrimination of one group of people against another. Like the one about Uganda a few years back. Everyone knew what was about to take place if the Asians were not rescued. It had been reported months before about the possibility of a genocide in Africa."

Mort's face was now expressionless as if something was finally reaching home. He continued, "People don't like the past being raked over. But it's our job to bring people or nations to accountability when wrong doing is done to the people they are elected to protect. The facts must always speak for themselves. I'll leave it at that. Frank will discuss ethics with you over the coming weeks."

After a quiet pause, Mort continued in a low voice, "You get my drift. Audiences become very emotional. Very committed to getting the truth out one way or another. And sometimes wrongly and sometimes rightly. And sorry to say, and often as not, people become very angry about these types of independent films. Human issues that are often raised firstly in the press, by say a deeply committed investigative journalist, seeking a good old story with a balance of truth.

"I hope you now understand better the responsibilities towards the public your role will have in the future." All the time Mort was very serious whilst he was speaking. "And as for Louisa, she's done some pretty daft things in the past but nothing like this."

Both Evie and Frank looked at each other as they both instinctively felt Mr Mortimer's concerns about his daughter's disappearance. Who, by now, had been missing for about five days and this was a growing concern for The Gazette. At the same time, shaking his head, he said irritably, "I cannot understand what possessed her to tackle the journalism of a short documentary the way she did."

He looked at Evie and asked, "Well, Evelyn, what happened last night? Take me through the incident, will you." With that statement, she handed Mr Mortimer her reporter's notebook and the notes she had made.

Mort took the notebook and flipped over the hardcover. Evie said, "They are recorded on pages 8-14. I number all my pages for reference's sake at the bottom."

Mort smiled at her. He read through the notes with an amazing speed and then returned his gaze on her. "Hmm. I can confirm that Louisa got the admin to book two seats on a flight to Belfast on Friday night, today in fact. One ticket in her name and one in yours." He looked directly at her whilst he spoke, always looking for any signs of anxiety or fear in the new reporter.

"And here's the rub," he continued. "I would like you to keep the meeting on Saturday. I want to know what Louisa was investigating with these two women. Frank here thinks I'm asking too much of you. Fresh out of uni and basically, no field work experience. Still very young, untested, untried, etc., etc. Frank has reminded me of all the reasons why I should not lay this one on you."

Frank looked at Evelyn and said, "Ms Borowski." Then halted for a few seconds. "May I call you Evelyn?"

The young woman answered quickly, "No, Frank, you can call me Evie." He returned her favour with a gracious smile; a side of Frank she had not witnessed in the last day or so.

"Well, Evie," Frank said. "I am apparently responsible for supervising your work just now. I inherited with Lou's blessing. Apparently, before she went off to London. So, after a lot of debate, what Mort and I have agreed is that we will leave it up to you. You met the two ladies briefly. What do you think of them? Personally, I really don't like it when the church, or in fact, any cult is involved.

"In my experience, it always leads to some form of trouble or deceit. Hence the appearance of the angry priest I suppose and his legal side kick."

The chief editor quickly retorted, "Frank, tone it down a bit. Keep it objective and don't let your personal feelings get in the way." Mort's voice was sharp and to the point.

Evie thought for a moment before speaking. "Well, the Taylors were very unhappy about Lou not turning up. And were also very surprised she hadn't. Meaning she had not altered any plans that she had with the Taylors. What stopped her? It was interesting that they referred to a piece of news copy, an article or something Lou had already written. And I would suggest that we need to find what that was all about.

"So, we can fully understand what is going on and perhaps where Ms Mortimer is at the moment?" Asked Mr Mortimer.

"Frank." Stopping in mid-sentence and turning her head towards Frank, Evie continued, "I certainly have no problem meeting with the two women. I don't believe they are a threat to me but they certainly riled that priest, Father O'Brien and the tall suited man with him. So, again my decision is yes. But I have to admit that I've never been on a plane before."

"I'm glad you said that." Mort fidgeted in his chair. "And the condition is, Evie, that someone goes with you."

Before Mort could say anymore, Evie interrupted, "My new friend, Claire, perhaps. She wants to be a script writer and she works or rather she is an intern at the theatre and works for Rachael. She is really knowledgeable about what goes on in that theatre. She knew about Lou and Rachael's so-called friendship…"

After a thoughtful pause, continued, "Truthfully, and in reality, Lou had apparently no time for the woman. A person said she just stroked her ego to get all the gossip. And apparently, Ms Cummins couldn't keep a secret to save her life!"

"Well, Lou has my sympathy on that subject," said Frank, "Racheal is a real piece of work. I know her parents and they're not much better. It's a wonder Doug hasn't got rid of her. All accounts are that she was useless."

Mort piped up, "I think she came to the post with a substantial donation attached to her ego. Mind you, that's all in confidence of course and doesn't leave this office."

At that moment, Mort picked up his mobile and rang a stored number. "Doug, is that you? It's Mort."

"Yes," came the reply.

"I'm going to put you on speaker for a minute." Mort explained the situation.

Doug said, "Sorry about Louisa. You must be worried sick. But regarding Claire, I don't think I've met her in reality. But yes, of course. I'll talk to Rachael now. No, I'll tell Rachael now to get Claire to come over to your office if she agrees. And I know what you and Frank are thinking. Rachael will agree or she can go home. Some donations are just not worth it. And again, Ms Borowski, thanks for making the theatre's position clear last night. Is that a Croatian name?"

"No, it's Polish, Mr Collingwood." He laughed and the call was ended.

"Right! I suggest that we regroup in the morning room at 11.00 sharp. We don't have much time to put this trip together. No field work to be more precise," Mort said, "And by the way, Evelyn, thank you. Anything that helps find Lou safe, I will be most grateful for."

Back in their office, Frank and Evie sat talking about the assignment and journalism in general. He opened the door and shouted across the jungle, "Hey, you come here." On that command, the young guy who was titled the paper's sports photographer came over to the door. Frank waved him in.

The young man's face showed a mixture of both fear and awe at the same time. He moved into the space that other journalists had overtime considered to be sacrosanct and out of bounds. The lad smiled and Frank returned the smile with a look of 'don't get too comfortable, son'.

Frank snapped, "The phone that Ms Borowski had been given by the Satanist in the basement…" At that moment, Evie picked up the phone and waved it in the air like a lollipop. As if speaking to someone who is not quite with it. Frank continued, "On it there is a tracking device or something like that. Isn't there?"

The young photographer confirmed that it would certainly work as a tracking device. He then simply advised, "You just have to turn it on."

Frank snapped back, "Well, turn it on then, Mr Photographer." The young man took the mobile from Evie and he navigated the menu swiftly and effortlessly.

"There you go," and handed it back to Evie.

"Are you sure it will work?" Frank asked for confirmation.

"As long as you leave it switched on. And as long as it is charged at all times."

"More to remember," Evie said under her breath.

At 11.00 exactly, Evie and Frank re-entered the glass bowled briefing room at the centre of the eighth floor. The room was full of senior reporters from the other columns. Claire, with her long red hair that she lifted up and moved away from her face, was there with a beaming smile. Evie sat next to her.

Claire leant over and, placing her hand over her mouth, asked, "What's going on? You want to see Rachael's face, I thought she was going to explode. Her face was the same colour as my hair. She asked me what was going on and I said I've been sworn to secrecy. It was brilliant to see her running around like a queen with no throne.

"I came straight over as Doug asked me to. I think her time is numbered. Christ, she had it all and still she can't find any decency in herself to treat people with some respect."

Evie gave her a quick catch-up of what was discussed that morning. "I asked for you to accompany me. Hope you're OK with that."

"What, are you kidding? A trip to Belfast to follow up a story? I feel great drama coming through all the time. A great mystery maybe. Those two old ladies left so quickly. Is it them we are going to meet?" She asked.

"Yes," replied Evie, still covering her mouth to ensure their conversation was private. At that point, Mort opened the meeting by telling the team of senior reporters what had gone down the previous night. He updated them on Lou's disappearance and how worried he was. All the time he spoke, there was a reverential quietness in the room, while they digested that they had lost one of their own, a member of the close fraternity of journalists.

Until Lou was found safe and sound, there was always the chance she was in a serious predicament, even in grave danger. It came with the turf for investigative journalists, who were some of the bravest people on the planet. None of what Evelyn was listening to now had been remotely addressed on her course, or even in her one to one's with her tutors.

She always felt something to be true in the great proclamation used in academic establishments, 'If you can't do the job, then teach it'. This musing was echoing around her mind at that very moment.

When Mort finished, the room rumbled into a round of clapping. It was a bit of a ritual at most papers when there was something dodgy a reporter was covering, usually related to some form of criminal activity or organised crime gang. They all applauded the journalists involved to show solidarity and support. At that moment, Evie realised that they were staring at her and Claire.

It made her feel so good for the first time in her crazy life, sort of respected. When everyone had been updated on what the other stories that were developing that day, and a nod from Mort, they all left the room in trickles, some still talking but all giving Evie and Claire a supporting nod or a smile.

It left five people in the room. Carol from the cave was present and reported that she had changed the flight tickets as instructed to reflect the new passenger's names. The flight departure remained at 18.30 today. She also confirmed that she had contacted the Manor Guesthouse.

Who she noticed replied immediately by email, and were more than happy to change the booking details to include a change of guest names. They now expected both Claire and Evie to be with them by about 9.00 tonight.

Carol continued, "You'll need documentary evidence of who you are before you board, even for domestic flights to Northern Ireland. We have contacted the usual hire car company, who have nominated a named driver to stay with you until you leave on the first flight back Monday morning. It's early; 6.30 from Belfast airport straight to Newcastle, so don't miss it.

"When you're out of the airport, a car will be waiting to bring you both straight back to this building where I presume, we'll convene the conversation where it has left off."

She turned to Frank and Mort before saying directly in front of the two young women, "It goes without saying, Northern Ireland has a history of not welcoming journalists to its shores over the last sixty years or so. So, stick to the business in hand, visit the women and stay locally at the guest house. No sightseeing or visiting the city pubs. The location of the hotel or B&B, not sure exactly what it is to be honest, for the description on their web site is very, very vague, but whatever it is, it's near the border.

"So again, you are just weekend walkers if anyone asks. Evelyn, whatever you do, don't display your reporter's badge. At the airport if anyone asks why you're there, it's for pleasure." Standing up, Carol from the cave on the sixth floor added, "Stay safe," and left the room. As Evie would recognise in the years to come, no one really understood the role of HR, but everyone has one, don't they?

Mort and Frank instructed Evie and Claire that they must phone from the hotel as soon as they arrived and to text at least twice a day to confirm that everything was OK, or to discuss any concerns or questions they may have. Mort reiterated that if Evie and Claire felt the least little bit worried or uncertain about anything at all, they were to withdraw, get back in the car and return to the airport, staying in sight of the public or better still the police at all times.

Frank leant on the desk. "I don't like this; bloody Northern Ireland, I ask you."

"You two girls go home and pack enough things for three days and then get back here for around 3.30. A car will take you to the airport," Mort instructed. They left the building and again Claire offered to drop Evie at the flat. They parted at around 12.30 and agreed Claire would meet her back at the office of The Gazette.

Back in the flat, Evie was happy to see Stig. She told him of the plan to visit the two old Ms Marple type characters and hopefully to find out what was really going on. She went into her bedroom to get ready, looked at the two suitcases standing upright in the corner of her room. "Stig! Help." He arrived at the door way of her bedroom. He immediately understood her predicament.

In a few seconds, he returned with a medium size holdall that he handed Evie with a smile. "Don't lose it. It's my favourite, Ms Borowski from Hull!" Adding "By the way, your phone rang but I never answered it." Instinct told her it was Lizzie. She had promise to call her when she arrived. Two days later, and she still had not done so. She picked up the old phone and rang her.

Stig moved back to watching the big telly in the sitting room. Evie shut the door and talked endlessly to Lizzie and told her everything that had happened in the last forty-eight hours. As always, she pictured Lizzie clapping her hands with excitement as she does.

Then after exchanging goodbyes with salutations of love for each other, she hung up, but not after agreeing she would phone her after work on Monday. She quickly sorted out the few things she needed and placed them in the holdall that Stig had lent her. She was ready in no time. Evie looked out of her window towards the park and it looked so inviting with the warm invisible blanket of mid-afternoon heat caressing the families as they played.

The well cut and trimmed grass looked cool and the leaves on the trees that somehow knew, as only nature can know, that autumn was around the corner. So, the old trees held their leaves out and pointed them upwards, grabbing the last moments of summer. Some cultures believe that the trees are pointed towards the universe so the earth can speak out to it.

The leaves on the Limes did look exceedingly beautiful and shiny, reflecting the sunlight out to all those that could be bothered to see it. Evie just smiled, loving nature at that moment and all that's good about it.

"Stig. I have an hour before I need to go back to work. Let me treat you to a cup of coffee in the park."

Stig looked at the clock and said, "Ok, I'm due in at 4.00. Got three ladies coming in tonight who I need to make beautiful for a wedding tomorrow morning."

Evie snapped, "I still can't believe you're a women's hairdresser."

They continued with the banter as they crossed the road and entered the park. Evie chose the same table she sat at before, but now with Stig opposite her. The fountain looked picturesque in the invisible yellow sunlight. The water cascaded down into the pond like pure wriggling life itself; a trickle of unstoppable sun-kissed sparkling energy.

Drinking coffee, they continued to learn more about each other and their individual paths they had walked to get where they were today.

Later on, the unflappable Stig gave his flatmate a lift and dropped her off outside the Evening Gazette's building. Clutching the holdall, she waved him off again. "This is quickly becoming a habit, Ms Borowski," Stig shouted out of the window.

Chapter VI
The Manor Guesthouse

Who controls the past…
controls the future.

Eric Arthur Blair

By 7.30 that evening, Claire and Evie boarded the domestic flight to Belfast and were drinking tea brought to them by a lovely steward named Rajnesh. They chatted about their hopes, dreams and aspirations, and all their favourite actresses that they liked from the days of the silent movies. All this seemed a game to them.

Then after a while, their minds turned back to the words that Frank had said to them before he saw them both safely into the taxi outside The Gazette. "Remember, this is work not a weekend off," he said sternly. "Be serious at all times and if people ask you questions, wonder why they are asking. Don't take any risks but try your hardest to find out what you can about what Lou was working on. But do not put yourselves in danger."

He then slammed the door to the taxi and with a gruff look on his face, moved back on the pavement. Claire leant over to Evie and said quietly, "I think he actually cares about us."

The theme of risk had been central to the day's events, firstly in the briefing room, then in Mort's office; and from Doug on the mobile. Even the crazy cave woman from HR on the sixth floor, and lastly Stig, all told her to be careful. She smiled and looked into her old purse, her mother's favourite when she was alive.

Inside, and folded neatly, was the two hundred pounds Frank had slipped her from the petty cash. She had never seen a fifty-pound note before, let alone had one, and here she was with four of them.

The plane landed on time at 8.20. By the time they alighted, it was nearer to 08.40. They walked into the domestic arrivals area and a man was holding a board high into the air with 'Ms Borowski' written on it in large letters in thick black writing. She walked up to him and introduced herself. Without speaking, he took out his pass and showed it to her, holding his credentials up to her face for inspection.

Claire stood next to her and listened to the man with the thick Irish accent. He asked her to text her company with his pass number on his badge for their security. He explained the paper would expect it and then they would pay the hire firm. What is it with badges, thought Evelyn. Everyone either wanted to show one or wanted to see one.

The hire car and its occupants pulled away, left the airport, and joined the three-lane motor way. The driver, looking into his mirror at the two women in the back seat, said, "They would be there in about fifty minutes." After this, he never spoke again. Given the time of day, the sun had now dipped behind the steep granite hills and high fields to the right-hand side of the car.

They were soon travelling along quiet country roads lined on both sides with hawthorn and elder that had been layered into neat hedges through the decades. On the hillside, you could make out scatterings of sheep that were chomping away at the tough clumps of hill grasses, oblivious to their futures. The two women minimised their conversation, as they had previously agreed on the plane, and by doing so, they were actually reinforcing what Frank and Mort ruled.

And this included the taxi driver, even though he showed them credentials which they never doubted were genuine.

Before long, they drew up in front of the large country guesthouse that was served by a large drive way in front of the house. On either side were lawns and mature cypress trees that were regimentally spaced. The grounds in which all this sat were surrounded by high granite walls made of large blocks of quarried stone.

The circular driveway was covered in greyed-white sparkling gravel that lit up slightly as the headlights reflected on them and guided the vehicle as its tyres crunched along. They climbed out of the car and immediately the large door to the house opened. The two ladies that they had met in Newcastle just the previous evening were standing on the large terraced porch to welcome them. Behind them stood two young women, who looked even younger than Evie and Claire, probably in their late teens.

"Welcome, and thanks for coming over at such short notice." The two teenagers automatically moved towards the visitors from England and took their bags and would take them to their rooms.

Evie answered, "Well, thank you. We all must have lots to talk about."

With this loaded comment, the tall woman, who was still dressed as she belonged to an era before the war, smiled back and added, "We most certainly do, Ms Borowski." She continued, "We put dinner back, so if you would like to freshen up in your rooms, dinner will be served in about twenty minutes." Dinner will be served! They both thought. Both Claire and Evie glanced at each other.

The formality seemed a little outdated for these two young and modern professionals. They were, what could be described as, two go-getters who ate most meals from a tray perched on their knees in front of their laptops or TVs. On the way to their rooms, they passed the large elegant dining room where they would eat tonight.

In the rooms, the bags had been neatly placed on the beds. A single room for each woman had been allocated. They quickly washed and stuck on fresh tops, liberally spraying clouds of deodorant over themselves. There was a knock on the door and Claire was standing there as Evie opened it. Claire never waited for an invitation and stepped inside her new colleague's room.

"How are you going to play it, Evie?" Claire asked.

Evie frowned back. "Well, I'll just ask her about the article Lou had written and why they were surprised by Lou's absence. That should open the door to Q&As."

They walked along an exquisite oak half-panelled corridor; the floor was adorned with a long red and black pristine Persian patterned rug that ran the whole length of it. The inner wall opposite the regency-styled windows was lined with a row of beautiful watercolours representing scenes they guessed of the local land and seascapes.

In the corner of each picture was penned the artist's name in fine white coloured brushed script. It read R. E. Esaw, the same signature was in the right-hand corner of all the paintings and just above the gold frame. For some reason, and given Claire's background in Fine Arts, the name drew her interest and her dark brown eyes moved closer to the paintings for a more detailed examination.

For a moment, she thought that they maybe originals. The artwork was exquisite. "No! They can't be. But they certainly are not prints." They carried on walking. After a minute and descending two flights of circular sweeping stairs, they found themselves at the opened double oak doors leading into the dining room.

A large table that had been set for at least twelve people ran the whole length of the room. Two ornate chandeliers threw a pale rosy soft light across the room that cheerfully invited the two visitors. As they entered, the tall woman that Evie had spoken to the night before moved towards them and introduced herself as Ms Edith Taylor, proprietor of the Manor Guesthouse.

"This is my twin sister, Ms Enid Taylor, but not in looks and features as you can see for yourselves." She turned her head towards the other woman who responded with a sweet smile and a sort of curtsey nod.

"There are only nine in tonight for dinner," Edith updated. "The colonel and the writer are eating out at a friend's house over the other side of the valley. But hopefully, you'll meet them tomorrow. The colonel is an interesting chap. Lived in India for about twenty years. Ex-colonial type you know." Ms Taylor continued, "Please, can you sit at these two seats." The other long-term guests were already in their usual seats.

"Creatures of habit are people. Don't you find that in investigative journalism?" Ms Edith Taylor threw the comment at Evie.

"Well, I guess some people are and some are not. I suppose it depends on your personality and character to some extent. And of course, your background." Claire looked at Evie and wondered where she got the quick response to these deeply complex leading questions.

Whilst moving to the two allocated seats at the end of the room where the doors were, others were settling in their seats. Leaning between the two women's heads, Ms Edith Taylor, the taller, and with a lightly touching hand on each shoulder, asked politely that they now leave the business of journalism until the morning. She did not want to upset the other guests with strange conversations around a short documentary that was not even shown. She said finishing up with "Do we?"

Evie turned her head and replied for both, "We do not. Do we?" Evie was used to people using language to make their unspoken statements. The taller of the twin sisters then moved down the room to take her seat at the head of the table. She rang a bell and in unison, the two young girls walked in and started serving dinner. Wine was offered but both Evie and Claire declined.

In fact, Evie had never taken a drink in her life. A part of the long-term plan that she had agreed with Lizzie. As for Claire, she seemed to follow Evie's lead in everything social and was reminded by the words of Frank, *we are at work*. After all she was here as a guest of the Evening Gazette or that's what she thought; and wanted to be in the paper's good books in the future. She, like the others, also had her own long-term plan to focus on.

As they ate the most wonderfully cooked food and roasted vegetables, followed up by a summer pudding and single cream, Evie looked about the table curiously trying to remember their names and job titles as each were introduced to her. Maurice was a very old, smartly dressed gentleman who had been at the guesthouse for as long as both the Ms Taylors could remember.

There was also an artist who specialised in landscape scenery; a female writer who specialised in feminist topics; and other guests who were tantalisingly introduced as 'Interested parties in the works of the Manor'. *Whatever that meant*, thought Evie.

About an hour and half later, and after coffee, Ms Taylor, the taller, suggested that they must be tired after such an exhausting day. They agreed and stood up and thanked everyone, and wished them all well before retiring to their bedrooms. Both Evie and Claire noticed that all the guest's eyes were on them. Not in a good night way. More of a staring way that was questioning their reasons for being here.

Back in their rooms, the women exchanged notes on the evening. They both agreed that the gaze at the end of the night made them feel a little uncomfortable and uneasy. Surely, they could not be in danger here at the Manor Guesthouse.

By this time, they were both back in Claire's room. Evie already had her reporter's notebook out and was recording the events of the day. She felt that by recording them in detail would somehow in the future, lead her to the sub-text being played out secretly around her. She was here to find an explanation for what had happened to Mr Mortimer's daughter. Or that's what she believed. The person who had given her the internship.

Just then, there was a knock on the door. Claire opened the door to find one of the young girls who met them on the porch when they had arrived, standing outside. The women had noticed that the girls had both proved to be first-class waitresses, noting that they handled the silver serving spoon and fork with great dexterity when serving the dinner.

"Good evening, I've come to turn down your beds if that is OK." Neither Evie nor Claire had the slightest understanding of what she was talking about but just said 'Yes'.

The young servant moved towards the bed and pulled back the heavy green patterned throw covering the bed and folded it neatly back. She then levelled it out and asked if they needed anything else. She said goodnight and moved along to the other rooms where she would carry out the same routine nine times.

"Turn down your bed," Evie said. "Is that what posh people do?"

Claire turned towards the bed and smiled. "It does look nice though and I could certainly get used to it." Both women then chuckled together.

Evie added, "You're incorrigible."

Just then, there was another knock on the door. Again, Claire answered it. It was Ms Taylor, the elder, with Enid a couple of paces behind her. She went on and thanked them for their understanding around confidentiality and privacy. She told them that breakfast started at 08.30 and that they should all meet at 10.30 in the library. The colonel will be joining us and we can discuss the incident that happened last night in Newcastle and the event leading up to it.

"You need some sort of explanation. I would imagine your boss, Mr Mortimer, has some questions he needs answering himself, and I guess that's why he sent you here. So, until tomorrow morning, we wish you good night."

Claire, after thanking them, closed the door. It was now after 11.00. Evie and Claire both settled down in their respective rooms and climbed into bed. Evie had opened her ringed notebook at a new page and with two 2B pencils started to write away furiously, like there was no tomorrow. She wanted to record everything precisely as it happened for Mr Mortimer. Instinctively, she knew it was expected of her and Frank had confirmed this but not in so many words.

Tomorrow his daughter, Ms Mortimer, and the article she was about to print would be the main topic of conversation. She lay there thinking what could be so controversial in a short documentary that the church took such great exception to it. Even obtaining an injunction to stop it being shown. And where is Louisa Mortimer? She asked herself the same question again, "How could a journalist just disappear off the face of the earth?"

About 12.30, she switched off the light and collapsed into a deep sleep.

Chapter VII
Why Is Nothing Simple?

Where have all the courageous men gone.
They're here but now they're women as well.

In the morning, the two young women went down to breakfast. It was held in a specific breakfast area towards the back of the Manor Guesthouse and next to the well-kept lawns with its own croquet pitch. A large glass hot house ran adjacent to it and was full of large exotic and very green tropical plants. Plants that she had to acknowledge to herself were in a much better condition than the jungle on the seventh floor of The Gazette.

Breakfast was a self-service affair, so both women felt at ease serving themselves. They spoke about the young girls who had waited on them yesterday, and how they felt a little awkward, to say the least, about all this high browed upper-class hocus-pocus.

After breakfast, and at the time arranged, the two young women wandered along the corridor to the library. At the same time examining the many pieces of antiquities and arts on display as they moved along slowly. When they eventually reached the old library, they found it was a large affair with many shelves filled with books that had striking titles on their colourfully leather-bound backs.

Ms Taylor, the taller, was already seated on a chair next to a coffee table. They both noticed that she was not accompanied by her sister, which was surprising to Evie and Claire as they had previously joked that the two sisters were 'joined at the hip'.

Instead, seated next to Ms Taylor was a smartly dressed young man. Evie quickly recognised him as Mr Mark Lister. The two women quickly joined them, full of anticipation of finding out what exactly was going on.

One of the young girls came over and asked if anyone wanted anything to drink. Both women said that water would be fine. The man had an herbal tea and

Edith declined all offers. After drinks had been served, Edith waved the girl away and told her to close the doors behind her. Evie noticed that Ms Taylor had a way of engaging people, which when she instructed someone to do something, no matter how softly and kindly she spoke, the instruction was always quickly followed by complete compliance.

Ms Taylor introduced Mark Lister and told them that he had been the editor of the short documentary that was due to be shown the other night. He also had a personal reason to be at this meeting. He and Ms Taylor left that comment at that and returned to the business in hand. Both girls said hello and then introduced themselves.

Ms Taylor and Mr Lister relayed the events that had led up to the evening in Newcastle. They had for a long time been trying to show a short documentary they had produced along with other people. If shown, it would have exposed various religious parties as war time collaborators with the German National Socialist party in the last war.

Evie said, "You mean the church when you say various religious parties." As soon as she said it, Evie realised that it was again a rhetorical question.

Without responding to the journalist's line of questioning, Ms Edith Taylor continued, "In the South, and in Dublin especially in the 1930s and 40s, there was still much bitter hatred and hostility towards the British colonial government." Edith stopped a moment reached for a glass of water and took a sip. "And for good reasons in many cases. You may not agree of course, given your history.

"Many republicans felt sold out and that the six counties rightly belonged to the new Irish Republican Free State. A United Ireland was always their ambition and it still remains so today for some." Again, Edith took another sip of water, drew breath and continued, "The documentary to be shown was about how some religious orders and various British Fascist parties would work together to help undermine British sovereignty after Herr Hitler and his thugs had taken over Britain."

The mood in the library was a sombre affair and Edith was struggling emotionally as she shared the events surrounding a programme called the Lebensborn Project. At this point, Mr Lister spoke, "There were many other things going on at the time as well. Well-planned things that were not only being developed but also put into place. They were just waiting for Churchill to be killed.

"Parliament to be replaced by a Nationalist Socialist Party. Many Irish gloated at that prospect and many ideological republicans were quite happy to jump into bed with the likes of Herr Hitler, Mussolini, Mosley. With the hope of eventually becoming a member of the Axis group."

Mark Lister took a moment and then continued, "That's why we had chosen the Art Deco Theatre's independent film festival to expose the truth that lay behind one of the darkest kept secrets about the Nazi plans for the post invasion of Britain. Especially the use of the Lebensborn Project which started in 1935 and was operational in at least eight other countries that were Nazi-occupied.

"There is evidence that the Lebensborn Project was implemented in a different format in Britain from 1942 in a secret operation." Mark Lister stopped there.

"You see how important the documentary was to us." Edith stood up at that point and walked to the back of her chair. "It was evidence of its existence. And after the showing, Louisa Mortimer was going to run a spread about the Lebensborn Project and how it has impacted on Britain in the post-war years. Even today." There was a moment of silence as the two young women took onboard the enormity of what was being said.

She paused again looked out of the window and then continued, "Claire, where do you think the can of film will be right now?"

At that point, Mr Listed interjected, "It was on celluloid film that had not been digitalised or copied yet. It's important to us that we get it back at all costs." There was desperation in his voice.

Evie leant forward in her chair and asked in her astute probing way, "Why this particular theatre?"

Ms Taylor looked towards her. "You do ask clever questions, my dear. Louisa was right about you." She continued in a quiet voice, "Why? Because we have tried in the past to get it shown at so many independent theatres' film festivals. But we have always been thwarted at the last minute. A mysterious fire, threats to owners, large sums being deposited in a curator's bank account. And so, it goes on."

She followed on, "Why we chose the Tyneside because, and to be quite frank, firstly it does not get a wide coverage in the national newspapers. We thought we could just slip the story in under the cover of showing it at a city that draws little attention to itself in reality. Secondly, the people who are trying to prevent it being released are always one step ahead of us.

"And thirdly, your Ms Rachael Cummins, the operations manager of planning is in all sense and purpose a meddlesome fool. We found she never examined the films before they were shown. Perhaps, and in her defence, and in this case, it may have been because it was produced using the German language with very few subtitles that were in Latin."

Ms Taylor, who was still staring out of the window, went on, "Racheal we gathered would never look for any ethical concerns or reasons for not showing a film. Or documentary by the look of it. And if she did, would she have the sense and integrity to challenge such material being shown. We were not so sure she would. And in fact, she didn't, did she? So that's why we chose the Newcastle venue, Evelyn."

"So where is the film now?" Edith said looking at Claire. "We would very much like it back," she asked in a quiet and appealing voice. Claire thought for a moment, nodded at Edith, and then picked up her mobile. Edith went to interrupt her but Claire put her finger to her lips to silence her. Edith decided to go along with Claire's directions.

She rang a number. It rang twice and it was answered by Geoff in the basement. "Hi, Geoff."

He recognised her voice immediately. "Hi, Claire, where the bloody hell are you?"

In a rushed voice, he said without taking a breather, "Miss Clipperly Clogs, the nickname the volunteers had given Rachael, is like a headless chicken. She's fuming that Doug let you go. In fact, she's missing today. A Saturday, I know."

"Geoff, I want you to slow down and listen to me and do me a big favour."

"If I can, Hinny," came the response.

"There's an independent shorty from the Thursday night showings. You remember the first night."

Geoff interrupted, "Can hardly forget it. With all that raucous happening on the stage and me with my fingers on the start switch."

Claire butted in, "Do you have the film and the can in the cellar with you still? The one that was titled 'The Lebensborn Project' or 'the devil's pact'. Or something like that?" She could hear him shuffling and rattling the film cans around in the background. Then after a moment, "Sure, it's here. A small can; can't be longer than twenty minutes judging by the length of film."

He then described the metal film canister. "The can is four inches wide and one and three-fourth inches deep. By the look of the mental tarnish and scratches,

I would suggest it is very old. It has an orange label with KODAK VERICOLOUR written on it in capitals. There is a long serial number and it's dated 1947.

"That's the one," a very relieved Mark Lister announced.

"That's great, Geoff. What I would like you to do is to take it home with you tonight and keep it safe for me until Monday when I get back. Some friends of the Evening Gazette need it. In return, they are going to give us some good space in the 'What's on section'." Claire gave Evie a sarcastic smile.

"But, Geoff, listen; whatever you do, don't pass it to Ms Cummins. She'll probably lose it."

"You have my word. I'll pass it to you personally on Monday morning."

"And, Geoff."

"Yes," he replied.

"I think you all do a great job in the basement and cellar."

"Thanks, Claire. Finally, someone who appreciates us film trogulids."

"But, Geoff, remember look after that film and tell no one you have it," she reminded him again, just in case, all the time the others listened intently.

"Will do, Claire, and bring us back some rock by the way."

Claire ended the call and put her mobile back on the table.

Both Mark Lister, the documentary producer, and Edith Taylor immediately thanked her for what she had done. "One of my people will collect it on Monday morning from The Gazette's office I would suggest."

Evie interjected at that point, "You'll pick it up from the Evening Gazette's office. I think we are entitled to a little private showing. The material and film are certainly rattling someone's cage."

Edith looked squarely at Evie and for a moment thought it over in her head. She leant over and whispered something to the man beside her. "All in good time, Evelyn. And not before you find Louisa." Edith sounded very cagey and it was obvious it wasn't up for debate. At least not yet, Evie thought.

"What about Louisa then?" Evelyn asked. "Where is she? You seem to know so much about everyone."

"In all honesty, her disappearance is as much of a surprise and disappointment to us as it is to you. I'm sorry, I can't help with that one. The arrangement was we would meet her, and I might add you as well, on Thursday afternoon at a cafe on Northumberland Street. We waited for three quarters of an hour but she never showed.

"She knew the documentary was going to be screened that night. In fact, she watched it with us and together we wrote an article which she took away. We were going to discuss the way forward at the meeting."

Evelyn looked at the woman and Mark long and hard to seek out any signs of hesitation, or untruths, shall we say. Evie thought at this moment, *We shall have to take her on face value.* The old trait inherited from care came rushing forward. Trust no one on face value. People often say one thing and do the other. Evelyn would keep her powder dry for a while, or at least until she had reported back to Mort and Frank.

"Well, hopefully, by Monday evening, the precious film with its unique evidence will be back in our safe hands," said Edith with a mutter of hope.

Evie's ears picked up. "You say evidence."

"Oh, yes. We have many people who have come forward to share their stories of what happened to their families between 1935 and 1945 in England and Ireland. Especially their Aryan looking daughters. And all in the name of the Fuhrer and the Father." With Mark's insistence, the group decided to leave it for now, as no more could be achieved, and they all agreed to speak again tomorrow morning in the library.

The meeting lasted about an hour and a half and by now, the two women found themselves sitting in the breakfast room trying to take in all that they had just heard and to make sense of what it meant. Alina, the older of the two Polish girls, appeared with a tray. "Would you like tea, coffee or soft drink?" Claire and Evie both said yes in unison.

Alina returned in no time and poured the tea and coffee for the women. "It's a rare day outside," the young waitress said. "You don't get many sunny days like this in this area." It was strange to listen to the Polish girl speaking in pigeon Irish. "If you don't have anything to do after lunch, I would say you should take a nice walk. The air is so clean up here in the mountains and the views are lovely when the sun shines out over the ocean."

Alina indicated with her head the direction they should take.

Claire and Evie decided that they would go for a nice long walk in the countryside and take some fresh air that afternoon. Both agreed they would have lunch first. The two young women went back to their rooms and changed into jeans and pullovers in anticipation of the walk. Evie texted Frank and Mort to say they were both safe and were going out for a walk. They would check in again later that same night.

After lunch, the two found themselves by the back door of the Manor House. It was around 2.00 and there was still some eight hours of daylight to be had. They looked at the hills in the distance, then noticed the two young Polish girls having a sly cigarette by a shed. The girls waved them over.

They introduced themselves. The younger girl who was nearly nineteen was call Izabela, or Iza for short. The older girl was Alina, and she was a little older but still only just.

Alina gave Evie a puzzled look. "You have a Polish name but an English first name and accent."

Evie thought, *Thank goodness for that, someone actually knows my name is Polish.*

"Yes, my dad was a Polish trawler man who worked out of Hull for a couple of years until he was deported or something like that."

"Why are you both here?" Claire asked. "You're not from around here."

"No," Alina said. "We came from Krakow originally. We were promised a modelling career in London. The man we met in Krakow was so charming and believable. He could have charmed the birds out of the trees as we would say in Poland. Our families signed all the forms as we were not eighteen at the time.

"But when we got to London, the handsome boy was not to be seen. We were taken to a horrible flat on the outskirts of London and it soon became quite clear what we had been brought here for. We tried to hold out but these people smuggling gangs can grind you down, day after day with ruthless threats against you and your family at home. Then they started to give us drugs of some kind and then it was only time.

"They had a client list of many Eastern European businessmen that hired you for the night. Sometimes if you weren't hired, they would stand you on corners and men would drive up, open the window, and eventually you got in. All the time the gangs watched you, day and night, cameras all over the building. In all honesty, we thought we would die here as whores.

"The gang members also threatened our families at home, telling them horrible lies about us. We had no way to escape, especially as some police were taking bribes to look the other way. We just kept praying to Mary, the mother of Jesus, for help."

"Then what happened?" Claire asked.

"Well, we were both working the Russell Square district. There was an Eastern European Entrepreneurial Event in London. There were lots of pick-ups about. The gang leader, a Pole, loved pick-ups. They always paid more. One evening, we were stood on a corner when a car pulled up. There were two women inside."

Alina continued, "My face was very bruised and my lip cut from being punched by a gang member. He said I was back chatting him. In fact, he was just a psycho like the rest of them. Why England allows them in, I don't understand. The woman in the car, the elderly one, said, 'Oh my dear, what has happened to you'. I smiled. I knew instinctively that they meant me no harm.

"At that moment, one of the pimps came across and started bad-mouthing me and the women in the car. 'You are ruining my business', he said in broken English and threatened the two old ladies. Well, at that point, the driver of the car, the man over there in the greenhouse..." They pointed to Clive, the gardener, who was well over six foot tall, very well built and looked nothing like a gardener.

"...Told him to move away. The pimp told him to mind his own business and get lost. At that point, Clive, the driver, opened the car door and, as quick as a flash, had him by the ear and was bashing his head of the bonnet. We were both just amazed and stood there in silence, it happened so quickly. The two women in the car never flinched or said anything. It was like it was something normal to them."

Alina was now fidgeting and showed signs of anxiety but continued, "We did not know what to do. We knew we were in trouble with the gang. They would blame us. Clive threw him onto the pavement, opened the passenger side door and said 'Get in', so we did. The two women smiled and said that part of your life is now over. We drove for about six hours and we slept in the car until we arrived at a port.

"The car drove onto the ferry and then was chained down. We all got out and the two women took us inside the cabin area with shops. One of which was a chemist and the two ladies took us inside. They asked the chemist to clean up my cuts and bruises. The chemist was very kind and a gentle person. By now, we were not use to that type of kindness."

She continued as the two young women listened intensely. "We went to a cafe on the boat and had some food. Real food and not what we were used to. It was lovely. Not the horrible soup but real food. I think I had a cottage pie and I remembered wondering how they would serve a cottage on my plate. I and Izabela knew we had been saved by these two gentle ladies.

"We arrived at the Manor House at around 4.00 in the morning and went to bed in a beautiful room with clean sheets and thick carpets covered the floors. We used the shower and the water was hot, and there was lots of bubbly soap. We pinched each other as we thought we were dead and had gone to heaven."

Claire and Evie stood engrossed and saddened by the story told to them by these two young girls. Evie understood that kids from care, especially young girls, could end up working for these ruthless gangs. And it has to be said some from Britain, some from Asia, and some from Eastern Europe. But they all had one thing in common. They had no morals or sympathy for the women which they blackmailed into prostitution or drug pushing.

And Evie knew first-hand, only too well, that vulnerable young girls after leaving care became easy targets because they generally had no one to look after them.

"So how did you get here?" Claire asked. "And are you safe now?"

"No! That was not the end of it. Someone snitched on us. A Polish guy was working on the ferry to Belfast. A couple of days later, the Polish gang turned up here! Would you believe it. We were terrified that we would be killed. Ms Taylor, who showed no fear, went out and spoke to them. The old colonel ushered us into the library and told us to get on the floor and sit in the corner. He produced a gun. It was mad.

"Ms Taylor spoke to the three men on the porch outside. She then made a phone call and apparently, an Irish man from Belfast spoke to the Polish guys. He had said they were on his territory and they were very much an inconvenience to him and had totally overstayed their welcome. Some other things were said which we have no idea about.

"Apparently, they just threw our passports onto the floor and shouted keep them. 'We can get another hundred stupid Pollak's like them if we want'. Ms Taylor never flinched once according to the colonel who was at the window."

Unbeknownst to the girls was that the big chauffeur called Clive, who had hit the gang member in London, was busy putting together a modern weapon in the greenhouse. At the same time, Rob, the other gardener who was busy hoeing the weeds between the flowering summer geraniums, was also placing his semi-automatic weapon on top of the freshly cut grass.

Apparently, the Eastern Europeans did not know that the colonel also had received a phone call about some highly unpleasant child traffickers being on the Belfast ferry and a description of the car they were travelling in.

Ms Taylor put the mobile to her ear and thanked the person on the other end. The local man spoke, "I think our debts are now paid and we are now just good friends, Ms Taylor."

The old woman replied, "Yes, but, Daniel, you know if you carry on what you are doing, you will eventually be killed by someone who wants your power and prestige."

"It's all part of the cycle of my life, Miss Edith. You and I know, I was born to die." Finishing with, "They won't trouble you or the girls any more. I would advise though that they don't go back to England or Poland for a time. Not until it is all blown over. And, Ms Edith, bloody-well stop taking in waifs and strays."

She replied, "And where would you be, Daniel, if I did?" The mobile went dead. She knew the number of the burner phone would now be useless and she would never have any further contact with the man from Belfast. A deep sadness passed through her at that moment. She recalled Daniel had been such a lovely boy when she and Enid found him behind some bins in the back streets of Dublin, an orphan.

"Well, that's how we found ourselves here," said Alina. "And take it as read, we will do anything for those lovely ladies. Anything! If you think we've been harshly treated, laying on service, lighting the Manor's fires, cleaning the piles of silverware, then don't waste your sympathy because we know real hardships and dangers."

Alina then changed the conversation, "Anyway, where are you two going?"

Claire pointed towards the hill. "For a walk up those hills like you suggested."

Iza and Alina both looked at each other and laughed. They opened the shed door and inside, there must have been at least fifty pairs of walking boots laid out on the shelves in it.

"We suggest you put some on. The bogs up there are horrendous and those things you're wearing won't last two minutes." Alina and Iza helped Claire and Evie choose the right size for their afternoon walk.

Chapter VIII
The Loving Spirits

Nowhere can a man find a quieter or
more untroubled retreat than in his own soul.

Marcus Aurelius, c.300

The two visitors took the girls' advice and put on a pair of boots each. Ten minutes later, they were walking casually up a country lane towards the steep slate-grey hills in the background. The hedgerows were bulging with berries of all colours, shapes and sizes. Autumn was approaching and the rose hips were in abundance. The women slowly walked in a meditative way and gossiped naturally, shared their life stories and spoke of their hopes.

A lot of their conversation was about the two young Polish girls and what they had just shared with them. Quickly, they understood how upsetting it was, and they agreed it felt best to leave it for now. They were just glad that someone had saved the girls' lives.

They walked on. Evie laughed saying, "Ms Rachael Cummins, you better watch out if you're staying around!" The young journalist quickly recognised that Claire had a clear career plan in front of her. One that involved her love of theatre and cinema. She smiled inwardly wishing her new friend of a few days all the very best.

Claire then laughed out loudly and retorted, "And the mysterious Louisa can watch out too. Hey girl."

"I don't know." Evie then halted for a moment to draw breath. "I've only met her on one occasion. But I do feel strange. Like she is saying something to me all the time through her written articles. And the way she always leaves the reader with a cute sub-text to follow in the closing paragraph. The things she has done for me like checking the flat out, paying the bond, she really didn't have to but she did.

"Why? And poor Stig, apparently, she really grilled him. Even on his moral conduct. And Louisa without really knowing me. Over the last week or so, it is a question that I have been struggling with! Why me?"

By now, the afternoon sun was graciously warming their faces. Above them, the deep blue crystal skies were to be seen in every direction. They climbed higher and higher, following the well-trodden old farming path. They reached a style, unbolted it and moved through it and bolted it after them. At that moment, they both looked across the fields behind them.

In the far distance, the Irish Sea could be seen. Best described as dark blue today and calm, not the usual threatening grey and green hurling sea they would have seen on most days from this advantage point. They turned and continued upwards at a leisurely pace, both young women engrossed in exploring each other's lives and backgrounds, with an ease that only mature friends who had known each other for many years would usually have managed.

Claire, who was amazed that Evie had been in the state care system, just looked at her slightly bemused. Evie was nothing like she had imagined a person who had been in care was like. Evie, who spoke with love in her voice, revealed that although, her mother who was her rock, she was also a very needy person. And even more so after her dad had been deported. She first turned to drink and then drugs.

She told Claire, "There is little chance that you can survive on a sink estate if you have the slightest emotional problems. You are either tough or you go under. Everyone seems to turn to the drink and drugs eventually. My mum was no different. Her downfall was her drug addiction and it eventually took her life."

Evie had never shared such stuff as this with anyone in her life so far, let alone someone she had only just met. Side by side, they moved slowly along the path, and Evie continued in a soft voice, "Social services tried their best but the writing was on the wall that I would be going into care. I must have been about nine or ten at the time and basically looking after my mum by then.

"Lizzie, our next-door neighbour, who had lived there forever, helped out a lot and took care of me. Her husband died with a little help from the shipyards and coal mines, of course! He had a bad back for many years and Lizzie had nursed him at home. They had lived at the same house since the end of the war.

"For the last twenty years, they saw what was happening with the amount of poverty and unemployment that was running amok. On the sink estates, there is not much chance of surviving life outside of them."

Evie continued and Claire listened intensely. Quickly realising that her life and Evie's was so different but they were so alike in character. Evie pointed out that her mum and her neighbour had a plan, that Lizzie would look after me. In reality, she already did.

"Mum went to parties most nights of the week, thanks to her so-called boyfriend, who was also qualified psycho. Mum cried all the time and kept saying sorry to me. Saying that when my dad gets back, everything would be alright. Well, he never returned and things got worse. The plan me and Lizzie made, the social services quickly put the kibosh on that.

"They said she was too old to look after me. I think Lizzie was in her late-sixties then and she is still going strong in her early-eighties. How wrong they were. The social worker explained that she felt I needed foster parents who could give me the help and support I needed. I still remember the social worker's face. I think she enjoyed her job actually.

"So, I was dragged away from everything I knew, including my home. My mum was crying her eyes out as usual. The street came out and the police had to intervene as the dead legs felt I was being kidnapped by the state. They all hated the social workers to begin with.

"I left but, on the proviso, I could see mum and Lizzie three times a week, which they grudgingly agreed. When my first contact was due to happen, it was cancelled. I was never told why. Then a few days later, these foster carers and social worker, who were all complete strangers, told me that my mum had died yesterday from a massive drink and drug overdose."

She described how the foster carer tried to comfort her and she pushed her away so vigorously that she fell back into a glass cabinet. "I didn't mean it. Apparently, from then on, and as I found out later, I was classified as a very needy child and aggressive. I eventually caught up with Lizzie, who said no one had contacted her about any contact. As far as I was concerned, they are pure liars you know.

"Then I was moved into a residential placement for an assessment and all over a period of about three weeks. What that was all about, God only knows. Being in residential was the worst time of my life. Lizzie kept visiting me and I kept asking why couldn't I live with her. Her house was empty. I would go to school and would behave. I would have promised those bastard residential workers anything to go home with Lizzie but they knew best."

It was the first time Claire had heard Evie swear.

"Enough of me, what about you?" Evie asked without looking at her.

She found out that Claire still lived with her mum and dad on the coast. They are both head teachers. She quietly added, "But they had forgotten the one child in the world that should be the most important to them." When Claire said this, Evie felt a sadness in her new friend's voice.

In reality, everything should have been perfect for Claire when contrasting her childhood to Evie's. But Evie understood intuitively why everything was not perfect for her. For Claire, her newfound friend, her unhappiness was because everything had to be perfect. People often forget, or to be more precise, fail to understand the impact and power of the parents' destructive need for perfection at times.

This meant for Claire that her parents were always forgetting her need of love by prioritising their own need of their child being successful. For Evelyn, she understood her mum loved her but was too weak in herself to prioritise Evelyn's care over her own personal and physical needs. But sadly, for the two young professionals this led them to the same conclusion about their completely different childhoods.

A form of unhappiness could arise from both good and bad intentions. A part of the strange subjective world we live in! Overall, these two young women, from very different backgrounds, found they had more in common than not. A position most likely their parents would not agree with if asked.

They had been walking for about an hour now. They followed another old farm path and soon found themselves standing in front of a row of old derelict farmer's cottages. Evelyn smiled to herself when she thought about the young Polish girl, Iza, who thought she would have to eat a cottage. They stood back from the road about fifty yards. In the front of the cottages were long narrow overgrown gardens, now full of weeds and long tuffs of marsh and meadow grass.

These gardens, once upon a time, would have been immaculate, and for decades would have provided these families with sustenance. The old windows were either broken or completely missing. Most of the roof slates were gone and birds flew freely in and out of the loft space that resembled a pigeon coup.

They looked around and wondered what life would have been like in those days for the tenant farmers. They cautiously walked down the path as all the gates had gone to the elements years ago. They peered through the glassless windows. Inside, the rooms were tiny compared to modern day standards. No furniture or signs that people once lived there could be found. The walls were soaking with damp.

The old iron fireplaces were missing, leaving just the old crumbled brickwork showing. They both tried to imagine how hard it must have been for the families up here in the wintertime. There were no trees to be seen so where did they get their fire wood from. They moved towards the last cottage on the left.

Suddenly, the door opened and out walked Maurice, who had been dining with them the previous night. In all honesty, he was as surprised to see them as they were to see him.

"Hello, Maurice!" Claire said in a cheerful voice.

Maurice doffed his cap and said, "Hello."

The women could see he was uncomfortable in their company. "Do you want us to go, Maurice?"

He looked up. "No, if you don't want to."

Claire asked, "What are you doing here?" Quickly realising it was a question that would be better coming from Maurice.

"I lived here once," he said timidly. "This was my mum's house."

They were a little confused about the whole thing. "We thought you lived at the Manor House with Ms Taylor and her sister."

"I do now. I live with Miss Edith Taylor. We were children together in the old days. I'm eighty-nine you know and still walk up here every day. One day, my mum will come back and my sister, Mary, too."

The two looked at each other curiously as they both concluded his mother must have died by now. He walked towards a gate at the side of the cottage. He opened it and asked if they wanted to see his flowers. In truth, they weren't sure what he meant. But the two of them moved towards the old wooden gate that was still working and peered inside.

The two were taken back to see what was actually growing behind the garden door. They moved inside the walled gardened area. Maurice was smiling at them as he knew they were lost for words; and more than just a bit. Maurice was quickly warming to these two young strangers. In fact, everyone was young in Maurice's eyes.

"Ms Taylor put the walls back for me as it was when I was a child. I grow vegetables for the Manor House. Ms Taylor thought it would be good for me to do something whilst I waited for mam and Mary to return."

Maurice continued to speak in a solemn voice. "Ms Taylor promised me she would find out what happen to my Mary. The youngest of eight of us you know. Dad had to take a ship to a new world where he could get a job and look after us. He died on the journey along with many others you know. One by one, my other brothers and sisters left home looking for work so as to support me and Mary but we never heard from them again. Ma worked every day at everything.

"Our neighbours then were just as poor as us. They all left in the forties when that big war was going on. By the end of the war, all the farms had been abandoned except ours. You can't grow much up here they said. Ma said it was just a big plan by the English. We stayed knowing Mary would come back to us. I'm still waiting for her."

"Where did she go?"

"The church people took her. Part of a big plan for the future of Ireland they said to ma and pa. They were deep believers in the faith of Jesus. The church ruled everything around here with an iron fist. If poor, you only ate if they approved it. They decided who married whom. Even who could go to heaven or not, but I waited."

Maurice looked up at the granite outcrops and mountain ridges. "If not here, they will return and live up there with the old spirits who will be kind to them, and look after them until we all meet again." The girls recognised sadness in his voice that came from the depth of his old soul.

"I hear my ma's voice in the wind sometimes. She still loves us all. She's been trying to find out what happened to Dad. The old Celtic spirits of the hills are helping her with that."

Maurice stood in front of the two young women, in his clean, dark blue pin stripped suit with turn ups on his trousers. On his feet was a pair of dark brown well-polished brogues. His wool knitted blue tie and old fashion styled button-down collared shirt were all well-kept and clean. Maurice saw the girls looking at him. "This is my gardening suit," said Maurice as he slowly swept his hand down the arm of the suit.

He continued, "Ms Taylor gets me one every six months. I have three now to work in. She says that we must all have high standards." He smiled and added, "She says I deserve the best for what we went through…"

He then turned his attention to the mystical garden. On one side was a long vegetable patch and on the other grew flowers of all kinds, shapes, sizes and colours. Maurice interrupted their thoughts, "I grow the flowers on this side as ma can see them from the tops of the hills."

Both girls stared in awe at the garden in front of them. Flowers of such beauty growing in the middle of this grey dank wilderness. It must have needed so much dedication and such a power of belief in what you are doing. The women found out that Maurice had been tending his mother's garden for well over sixty years. Ms Taylor had bought the derelict row of cottages.

And much to the disdain of the rich landowners, who conducted such clearances with such guile that they must have had been helped by the devil himself. Or apparently so, the old locals thought.

Inside the tall walled garden, the flowers were absolutely exquisite and quite breath-taking. If the land had been cursed at one time, then this walled-off garden must have been saved by Maurice's ancient spirits for a reason of some sorts, thought Evie. Apparently, no one had been here from the outside world except a young girl called Louisa for a long, long time. She came here with Ms Edith.

The two girls felt quite honoured by this fact that only about six people had ever seen Maurice's mother's secret magic garden. Tall fox gloves roamed in time with the music of the wind rolling down the hillside and over the tall stone walls. Marigolds flourished along the edges of the well-kept borders.

The deep and rich orangey red petals that surrounded the inner black eye of the flower head, undoubtedly looked back at you as if they were connected to your unknown soul, and never the other way around. The old pagan spirits would not have planned it any other way.

The time was now getting towards late afternoon. Maurice thought it would be best to start getting back down to the Manor. He picked up an old-fashioned garden basket full of various fresh vegetables. "For the cooks of the Manor House kitchen," he said proudly. Together, the three left and joined the paths that would take them off the hills. The sun now setting behind the taller peaks, threw rays of sunshine up into the evening sky.

They knew that behind them in the mysterious garden they had left some form of spiritual mystery which gave Maurice and his family a deserved peace. The flowers and vegetables gave him an eternal life cycle of birth, growth and death that was repeated for this old man and gave him the willpower to live on. As his mother would always say when they were feeling down, 'summer was just around the corner'.

On the journey back, Maurice named all the plants, the trees and birds that flew around them. Not only in English but in Gaelic and in Latin too. In the trees and hedges, the birds merrily sang a concoction of tunes to the three humans that were visiting their world and the secret domain of nature. Claire thought of Vaughan William's music 'The Lark Ascending', and how it would have been so suited to the here and now.

Maurice explained that his mother and her mother before her, knew the names of all the herbs, which the un-concerning eye would never see. His mother's secrets of all the herbs and what they could be used for were now sadly gone. He explained how she dried them in summer, made potions of them in autumn, and gave them willingly away to all neighbours in the winter and spring. His mother, Mary O'Connor, saw them as a product of the gods and not of men.

To be shared and given out to the sick on the hillsides, without man's religious prejudices butting in. The days back then were hard; death and infanticide just a part of hillside life.

The two girls listened deeply to Maurice's recollections and the natural beauty that this old man held in his soul. Maurice, from his experiences, knew that his life had reached the fourth and final movement of a long and tough symphony. Sooner or later, he would join the spirits on the hills, and then dance once again around a summer fire, as he had done so as a child with his brothers and sisters and all their friends; and not a pair of shoes between them all.

This brought him a warm feeling inside; not only was he ready in age for what was to come but also in the spirit of the old Celtic times. The depth of conversation meant that before they knew it, they were removing their boots and placing them back in the shed.

As they walked through the hallway and past the library, they caught a glimpse of the two Taylor women, Enid and Edith, the colonel, and another man that they could not make out. All were in a heated conversation with Father O'Keith and the well-dressed lawyer who were all at the Independent Film Festival's opening night. From a distance and through the glass windows, it was obvious that they were not in any form of agreement.

People were gesticulating with their hands and pointing at each other. One could only infer from the distance, and not being able to hear the conversation, that the two parties were blaming each other for something; and continuing an argument that had started at the theatre in Newcastle. Before they could take a breath, the two women still in the hallway saw the library's doors burst open.

The priest and the lawyer, who was quickly following in his footsteps, both stopped for a second and gave them both a look of disdain, dismissing them without even an acknowledgement.

One of the Polish girls tried to open the door for them, but the priest spat, "Don't bother, we'll find our own way out." He then opened the large front door, but before leaving, spun around and looked at the two English women. "Keep out of business that does not concern you!" There was so much intensity in his words that he was nearly hissing them as he projected his hatred towards them.

Before either could respond, the two men left the Manor Guesthouse, descended the steps and climbed quickly into a car that was waiting for them. A tall man in a dark suit shut the car door behind them, climbed into the front and they drove off.

Edith came out of the library and asked if the two women were alright. They both replied together, "Yes."

"Good," Edith replied as she retired back into the library closing the door after her.

"What was that all about?" Claire asked looking at Evie.

"I'm not sure but that priest sure looked pissed off about something."

They both went to Claire's room and spent most of the evening in it. Evie had the work phone out and was planning to text both Mort and Frank. Claire helped Evie with the device and showed her what it was capable of and how to work the apps. Also, she checked that the tracking device was still active.

They took photos of each other and selfies together. Messing around and recording the memories for each other. Both agreed at this point that no pictures or information would be placed on any social media platforms, now or in the future. Both young women had experiences of other people who had bad times with social media.

The rest of the day was uneventful, except of course for the incident that they witnessed after returning from the walk. Evie then checked in with both Frank and Mort and told them they were both OK, and were going to take a walk into the village and have a look around tomorrow.

They both went to their rooms for a shower and to get ready for dinner. Before they left their respective rooms, Iza, the younger of the two Polish girls, knocked on Claire's door. "Good evening," she said with a muddling of accents if truth be known. "Ms Taylor has requested that you join her in the library before dinner, she needs to talk to you both."

"Ok, no problem, say five minutes." At this, the young maid turned and left, walking swiftly along the red Persian rug with a measured step that most likely one of the Taylor women would have shown her.

Claire knocked on Evie's door. "Hi, Ms Taylor, the taller, would like us to join her in the library." Evie was already dressed. She picked up her notebook and pencil and the women joined the group in the library as instructed.

In the library, Ms Edith Taylor, the colonel, her sister, Enid, the shorter, as the two had nicked-named her, were sitting on chairs that were arranged in a circular fashion again. When the two women walked in, all stood up and thanked them for coming at such short notice. When they sat down, all the others sat down as well.

The young women were not used to being greeted so graciously and formally. "Would you like a drink or something else before dinner?" Both asked for water again.

The colonel looked at them. Well, to be correct, stared. He then inquired, "Is there any information about Ms Mortimer yet?"

Evelyn responded by saying, "No. No one has heard from her since early last week when she left for London. That was the last time anyone heard from her. As far as Frank knows…"

Ms Taylor, the taller, cut across her and asked, "Who is Frank?"

Evie continued, "He's the papers' racing correspondent. He's been with the paper for decades. And from what I hear, knew Lou since she was a kid."

The colonel moved in his chair and reached into the inside pocket of his jacket, removed a small notebook and quickly thumbed through the pages. "Yes, Mr Frank Cousins. Started his career with an Irish paper based in Dublin. Now a first-class reporter of the sport of kings. His tips had helped the dedicated racing man gain a good return. Well-liked chap but very caustic to many, if not damp-right rude."

Evelyn thought to herself, *They have him pigeon-holed.*

Edith Taylor then discussed various matters. She thanked the two women again for stepping in at the last moment, as they must have been more than a little bit confused, about all the going-ons over the last four or five days. She then said, "Before we part company, can we ask you to do one other thing? We have an envelope we would like you to pass to Ms Mortimer. She knows what's in it."

The group talked openly how they had been working with her on their short documentary but she must have been held up. Edith disclosed that Louise had actually been in London for an interview with a national paper. She never said which one, but it would have been an influential career move for her and us. Whoever 'us', thought Evelyn.

Edith continued, "It was one of the reasons she recruited you. As she did not want to leave her dad's paper without finding her own replacement. She felt a great loyalty towards the paper. She certainly saw herself in you. So would you take this envelope and pass it directly to her when you see her? At the same time, can we confirm that you will pass the short film to our agent who will arrive at the newspaper on Monday morning at around 10.30.

"After today, ladies, you'll not see us for a few weeks. Obviously, you'll have lots of interesting questions to ask. But if you could direct them towards Ms Mortimer when you finally meet her. From what I've heard, you will have a good start to your career at the paper. Always remember you'll know when you need to move. So just do it."

Edith turned towards Claire. "As for you, Claire, we haven't given up on our short documentary yet being shown. We feel that you will play a big part in the future development of the Old Art Deco. Our advice to you is keep going the way you have. Keep approaching your work in the same manner and things will then move in your favour. We are sure of that and very soon."

She continued, "At this point, we would like to wish you a safe journey back to England. We would invite questions but, in my experience, if I answer a question at this time fair and squarely, you'll be after me with many more. Would you not agree, young Ms Borowski?" She smiled at the two young women and with that, the meeting ended. Evelyn ran back up to her room and put the envelope straight into her bag, then returned downstairs for dinner.

Saturday night, they dined at the Manor again but there were only three other people at the table. The Taylor women and the colonel were out for the evening. Maurice was there with his lovely smile and Mr Mark Lister, who was in the library with them that same morning was very quiet and reserved, as he had been the previous night.

Both women knew it was not a night for small talk. Mark Lister was constantly looking at the screens of the two mobiles he had on the table in front of him as if he was waiting for some kind of response or spiritual inspiration. He was both fidgety and agitated by the lack of the response he was getting. Or rather not!

On the way out of the dining room after dinner, the two women bumped into the three leaving. The two Taylor women and the colonel were all dressed to travel. The other gardener, Rob, stood by the front door looking immaculate in his well-tailored jacket and trousers. He gave Evie a smile.

"Oh, you're going out?" Evelyn asked.

"We are, my dear, and we will not be back for a few days. So again, we say goodbye. And get Lou to ring us ASAP." At this point, Ms Taylor, the taller, walked towards the young women and put her hand on theirs lightly.

"I must say you were very kind to Maurice today. He really enjoyed the walk back with you. He'll remember it forever. He has had a very bad life but he is happy and safe here. Again, thank you for your sensitivity towards a lovely old gentleman. Not many young people have what you have."

They cordially smiled at each and then went their separate ways.

After the final goodbyes, both women retired to their rooms early so as to grab as much sleep as possible. Evie, through habit, recorded the day's events. She stared at the white A4 envelope leaning against her travel bag. Evie picked it up and wondered what was in it. She noticed the glue on the fly of the envelope was not fixed. It popped opened in her hands and she peered inside.

There were two sheets of A4 paper with lists of names on each one. About fifty names on each sheet of paper Evie guessed. She placed them separately on the bed thinking to herself, *I have to pass you on to Lou on Monday. She can deal with you and do whatever they had planned together. Where the hell is she?*

Evelyn stared at the names which meant absolutely nothing to her. At that point, she was about to pick them up and return them to the white envelope. It was then that it struck her that perhaps she could take pictures of them with her new wonderful mobile, just in case they were lost somehow. She said this to herself in a way to justify her actions later on.

In her mind, she reasoned that's exactly what Lou would have done. Well, she proceeded to take two pictures of the documents and slipped them back into the white envelope and then stuck them down properly. A few minutes later, Evelyn was tucked up inside the comfortable bed and soon sleeping soundly and contented.

Chapter IX
What Else Is There to Say?

Thinking is very far from knowing.

Old Proverb

Sunday was the last day they spent at the Manor Guesthouse on this occasion. In the morning, Evelyn took time trying to write up some notes and to formulate some ideas to present back to Mort and Frank. In the afternoon, the women went down to the village. They had planned to go into the city and do some sightseeing but they were warned to stay near the guesthouse and keep a low profile. So, this is what they both did.

In the morning, Claire had spoken to her parents and told them she was having a lovely weekend in the quiet picturesque countryside of Northern Ireland in the company of Evelyn Borowski from The Gazette. In the village, they bumped into the two Polish girls and decided to take a short stroll along the clifftops with them. The weather had not been so friendly on the Sunday in question but still all four enjoyed the brisk sea air.

The two Polish girls were so excited. The Taylor twins had arranged for their families to travel to Belfast, where they could spend a few days together to catch up and continue family life from where they left off. The girls were bursting with excitement and so looking forward to seeing their loved ones.

Before long, the two women were back in their rooms getting ready to return to Newcastle on the first flight out in the morning. After an early dinner, both women retired early so as to get a good night's sleep.

After catching the earliest flight out of Belfast and arriving on time at Newcastle Airport, and as planned, both women were dropped off at The Gazette's office in the centre of the city of Newcastle. They paid the driver in cash, for which Evelyn demanded a receipt, much to the annoyance of the driver it has to be said!

"Are you going straight to work, Claire?"

"You mean right now? Not a chance, Miss Evie Borowski. Leave you to your own devices at this crucial time? Never! And me having to miss my Monday morning irrational rant with the great princess Rachael. Who will undoubtedly be outlining what's happening this week, especially for me." Claire looked defiantly at Evie. "No. Not a chance. Anyway, I'm expecting Geoff to deliver the cellulite film to me here."

Both girls laughed at the sentiments behind Claire's decision. By now, it was 9.55 am. As they walked through the foyer, Maggie as always, was at her desk resembling a large crane whose neck was fully extended so that she could see over the computer she rules the world from. She looked straight into the faces at both girls and said, "You need to go to the fish bowl briefing straight away. It's on the eighth. Your friend here needs a pass."

Maggie slid open a draw and pulled out a temporary pass and handed it to Claire. This transactional arrangement was more akin to a person handing over the golden pass to delinquent children in the *Willie Wonka & The Chocolate Factory* movie.

"Thank you," said Claire placing the land-yard around her neck at the same time.

The crusty receptionist then ordered, "Sign here," and pointed to a visitor's book on the desk. "It's for the fire regs. You never know! Do you!" The receptionist said tilting her head in an old-fashioned school teacher way, to ensure that the fire register had been completed correctly.

"You certainly don't," replied Claire.

In the lift to the eighth floor, Claire asked Evie if she had a brief or something.

Evie's look said it all. "What? Are you winding me up? I have my notes from the weekend." For a few moments Evie questioned her own sanity to deal with the meeting but in seconds, she had recomposed herself. Her time in care had meant she had to deal with new and awkward situations at all times. That or sink into oblivion. And oblivion was never a choice for her!

By the time they arrived at the fish bowl, already assembled were Mr Mortimer, Frank Cousins and a woman from Legal who was going to advise and make notes of the meeting which was a part of the journalistic process.

"Hi, Ms Borowski, and I take it this is Claire. And I also take it she is joining us this morning. And yes, I've spoken to Doug." Claire looked at him inquiringly. "I know your boss at the theatre. He is aware that you are back safely. Remember, your boss has a duty of care for you, even if some bosses don't show it." Mort smiled and added, "Your family are aware that you are back, Claire?"

She replied, "Yes, spoke to them this morning. But thank you."

"Good. Shall we get started then?" Doug said. "Evie, and may I call you that?"

"Of course," replied Evelyn shrugging her shoulders to support her decision.

Mr Mortimer spoke softly but clearly, as he outlined to her that he and the paper, both realised that she had spent no time at all with The Gazette. And had no time to properly process the induction information and thank her for her co-operation and flexibility. Evie quickly realised that Mr Mortimer was choosing his words carefully.

Again, he spoke, "First of all, Evie, you've been here for less than a week. And in that time, we've asked you to fly to Northern Ireland and stand in for a reporter and follow up on whatever she was working on. A tall ask! And we must recognise this."

Evie caught Frank out the corner of her eye totally agreeing. Perhaps he's not as bad as he makes out, she thought.

Mort added, "Besides, and for the record and to update you all, I'm still worried sick about Louisa's disappearance. And to let you all know there has still been no contact with her by anyone. I know she's my daughter and she could act irrationally in the past but she has grown out of that type of behaviour. Thank goodness." Frank nodded in agreement.

Mort continued, "Claire, I spoke to your boss, an old friend of mine, who OK'd it for you to accompany Evelyn. So, on behalf of the paper, I would like to thank you for stepping in at short notice. Not everyone would have done that."

Claire could only picture Racheal's grating face at being overruled by her bosses. The assembled people took it that Claire's smile was a response to the recognition they had just given her.

"Back to what we know then." Mort looked down at some notes he had made over the weekend. "But before we start, Claire, I think it's best you return to the theatre." Both women looked at each other with surprise by this statement and a little concerned.

Evelyn replied, "With all due respect if you don't mind, I would like Claire to stay. She witnessed everything that has happened since last Thursday, and I may well have misread a situation or left out something that she could add too."

Frank, who was fully stretched out on the chair and with his hands clasped behind his head, looked up at the ceiling in disbelief. "This just gets better and better. Two interns! Can we not just get on with our jobs? I've got five hundred horses to cover tomorrow…"

Mort, now the chief editor, raised his voice. Then sharply interjected, "Frank, you're not helping. A reporter is missing and I want to know why! We've been friends for a long time. So, so either stick with me on this one, or you can leave now. I know she was working on something. Something I guess that was not quite her usual reporting area. That's what I'm guessing.

"I'm sorry to get Evelyn involved but she was already booked to go with Lou to meet some people, Lou already had contact with. That means Lou had thought things through before Evelyn's arrival last Wednesday. And I want to know what!" Mort looked at Evelyn and without saying anything, she knew intuitively it was her turn to talk.

"Well, I've made a list of facts that I've learnt." From the notebook clasped in her hands, she read the following out.

- Louisa Mortimer and the Taylor twins had met previously, that's a confirmation. They said they and Lou had already written a piece for the paper.
- On the day the film festival was to start, they had already agreed to meet at a cafe on Northumberland Street. I believe the meeting was to be between Ms Edith Taylor, Ms Enid Taylor. Louise Mortimer, and if I read the situation correctly, Lou was going to take me with her. That's what her calendar confirmed."
- Fact Louise Mortimer never attended the meeting.
- Fact the Taylor women were as surprised as everyone else about Lou's disappearance. They were sympathetic towards you, Mr Mortimer. But you could tell it had altered their plans somehow. Of which they were annoyed but hid it well.
- Lou had already written a piece to go alongside the short documentary that was to be shown Thursday night. No one, and I mean no one, has

- seen this copy yet. At this point, Evie added, "And I've poked around everywhere."
- Lou had already made all the arrangements to visit the Manor Guesthouse that weekend. And with me in tow as Frank would have put it. The arrangements were made well over three weeks ago. So, one can review that this was a strategic move, a planned event.
- Over the weekend, the long-term residents of the Manor Guesthouse were very hospitable, but at all times guarded around myself and Claire, with the exception of the two Polish maids.
- The two maids who worked at the Manor stated that they had been rescued from a child prostitution ring in London. I don't think this was a planned event, but one that the Taylors came across accidentally, and they found themselves rescuing the children through righteousness.
- The gardener come chauffeur is not who he appears to be. Also, the other gardener called Rob seemed very alert to everything that was going on around him. I would say they are both from military backgrounds given the way they hold themselves.
- The lovely Maurice, who adores these ladies, was at some time rescued by the Manor House mob in the past.
- The colonel is central to the decision-making process. Even though he gives the impression he is acting on the edge of everything. He strangely knew Frank's working biography in detail.
- The Manor Guesthouse (mgh@airspace.com) is an old colonial mansion dated from about the 1850s. It is in an immaculate state of repair for such an old building. Usually, people who own these places go on consistently about rising damp, the roof and letting the public in. I asked Maggie on reception to look at the booking procedure for the Manor Guesthouse.

Although, there is a web page, there is no booking system. I would suggest that the only way you can stay at the Manor is if you were invited to. I think in reality not many people are invited to stay. I would say it is by special invitation only.

The information about the documentary was sparse but it seemed to involve the Nazis and the Lebensborn Programme (meaning Fount of Life). It was conceived in 1935 and was headed up by Heinrich Himmler himself.

By now, Frank had sat up in his chair. The recorder was busy recording and Mort listened with his eyes closed as if in deep thought.

Claire looked at Evelyn with astonishment. The way she produced observation after observation about the last three days was something she had not expected.

"And by the way, the driver knew you both personally. He sends his regards, Mr Mortimer, Frank..." Evelyn nodded towards them.

In Mort's and Frank's defence, they disclosed, "To put it mildly, we were slightly worried about you both. Northern Ireland is a special place for journalists to be, especially baby ones." Claire wondered if Frank included her as the other baby journalist. *I would love that*, she thought.

At that moment, the intercom sitting at the centre of the glass table within the fish bowl crackled into action. "Margaret here. There are two gentlemen here, one for Miss Claire Smith, the other for Ms Borowski."

Mort lent forward. "Send them up. Eighth floor." Looking at the young women, "Who the hell are these people?"

Evie and Claire gave Mort and Frank a quick overview. "I think I need to speak to Geoff on his own outside of this meeting, if you don't mind," Claire informed those present. She left and met Geoff coming out of the lift and took him to one side. She acknowledged Clive, the gardener, and he was shown the way to the glass bowl.

Claire whispered to Geoff, "Have you got the spool of film?"

"Yes, here it is as ordered."

"And the digital copy Geoff?"

"Yes, as directed. It's in this envelope."

"And Ms Cummins knows nothing of this, Asked Claire. Not a dickie bird." Geoff replied winking at the same time like a mischievous school boy.

"Good, keep it that way. For me, Geoff, OK."

Claire directed that Geoff went back to the theatre and she would catch up with him in the basement later. Geoff left via the lift and strolled back to the theatre that he passionately loved with all his soul and body; and the unpaid job that he took so seriously, rescuing old film from the death of modernism.

Claire went back to the fish bowl. Doris, the legal secretary, made everyone a fresh drink and was offering out milk and sugar. Claire indicated by holding up the film in the air for all to see that she did have the canister and short film.

She placed it on the table and passed it to Mr Mortimer. All the time, Clive, the man from the Manor Guesthouse watched the proceedings with intense interest.

Evelyn broke the silence. "Hi, Clive, didn't expect to see you so soon. We met at the Manor. Clive's the gardener come chauffer, and many other things I expect," remarked Evelyn with interest. Clive, from the Manor Guesthouse, responded with a smile and a nod towards Evelyn.

"I'm here as instructed by Ms Taylor to pick up her film. Can I have it please? I know the ladies will be so relieved that it is back in safe hands."

For some reason, they all looked at Mort. Shaking his head, he asked, "Claire, does this film belong to these people and is it their property."

Claire replied, "Yes, undoubtedly. I was there when Ms Taylor handed it to Rachael for the showing."

"Well, give it to the gentleman then." Claire pushed the can of film towards Clive, who reached out and grasped it, and then placed it in an expensive looking briefcase.

"And the envelope you were passed by the Taylors to give to Louisa Mortimer. You have it safe. Yes?"

Evelyn looked directly at Clive. "Yes, in my bag still."

Clive asked, "You wouldn't mind if I see it then."

Evelyn looked towards Mort who opened both hands as giving his blessing. At this point, Evelyn opened her travel bag, or to be more precise, Stig's, and took out the A4 white envelope. "Here you go," said Evie.

Clive took the envelope and examined it. He looked up at Evie and smiled. "I see it is well sealed now…" giving Evelyn a knowing glance. "Ms Taylor and the colonel will be pleased you took such good care and interest in it." Evie knew that Clive's words were loaded.

He pushed the envelope across the table towards Mort. "I think you should hold onto this for Ms Mortimer. Incidentally, I met with Louisa twice. She had a spirit in her that lifted others around her. The Taylor twins thought much of her. They liked her very much, Mr Mortimer. And if we can assist you in any way in the future, you have the number of the Manor House. I will leave mine with Evelyn. I must catch my plane and get the film back to its place of safety."

Mort, who was getting a little tired of the games being played out, said, "Waite here a minute. Louisa was covering a piece about an independently made documentary. And before it's showing, she mysteriously disappears off the face of the earth. One minute you're saying she was thick as thieves with the people from the Manor and now you're saying that's an end to it. Not as far as I'm concerned." The recorder was writing frantically in shorthand to keep up.

"No. That is not what I'm saying, Mr Mortimer. Ask Evelyn, I think she knows why she was in London." At that, Clive stood up.

At the same time, Evie stood up. "I'll buy you a cup of coffee. It's the least I can do. I know your flight isn't till 2.15." Clive smiled at Evie thinking, *She is a smart one. Louisa was right about her.* Claire turned her head towards Evelyn and wondered how she knew this.

Clive turned towards her, looked at Evelyn for a few seconds, and knew instinctively that she would pester him all the way to the taxi. She had a look that he understood well enough, especially the determined ones. "Ok! A quick one. Say, for old times' sake."

Evelyn gave Mort a look as to say 'I know what I'm doing'. Claire automatically stood up as the invitation included her if people agreed or not.

After agreeing, Mort had one more instruction, "My office this afternoon at 3.00, young lady. I feel we need a conversation about what your job exactly is here. Wouldn't you agree?"

The three left the building again. Maggie was, as always, on the desk looking suspiciously at them as they left. *Wonder what the newbie is up to now? Bloody carbon copy of Louisa that one, if you tell me,* she thought to herself.

Frank and Mort stayed in the room after everyone left.

"Christ, Mort, you don't buy any this mystery stuff. Do you? It sounds more like they've been playing Cluedo at the Manor. Colonel Blink, Ms Taylor, Clive the chauffer, Polish maids…"

"Frank, please…" Mort continued. "What I know is my daughter hasn't been heard from since last Monday. She was going to London for a day. Why? I don't know. Like you, Frank, I have enough mysteries to deal with at the moment. And a paper to run."

Frank turned towards Mort. "Are you keeping Evelyn on? You know she'll be hard work."

Mort leant on the side of the chair and looked at Frank, their faces not even twelve inches apart. "Yes, Frank, I know she's trouble and Louisa knew that and now you know that. But we all know what makes the best investigative journalist. Don't we, Frank? Not the ones which roll over, take bribes and write enough crap copy to get their columns filled for their wages.

"Or is it that we've forgotten, Frank, that it's the ones that are obnoxious with their questioning, tenacious and diligent to a fault in their story writing. The journalist who cares about reaching a balanced story that is full of truth, that is weighted with both good and bad. God knows, Frank, even you must have realised that social media is now in the hands of the powerful capitalists and unfit politicians.

"You can hide away in your horsey world now, Frank, safe and sound, but how many times were you nearly killed in the old days so that truth could be shared with the reader. Yes, she is staying until at least I can find out what happened to Lou. She is a link in all this. And maybe unwittingly, but she is, Frank. Call it journalistic intuition if you like or just bullshit. She stays. And between you and me, I like her and so do you, Frank. I can tell."

Outside of The Gazette's office, the three people entered the Shack café. Old steel shipping containers that had been conveniently turned into street type bars and cafes which the professional Gordie city folk just loved to visit on Friday evenings. Clive looked around suspiciously and said, "This will be fine." The seating area was outside and, given that the lovely lunchtime crowd hadn't arrived yet, they were afforded relative privacy. A very young lad came up to them and they ordered three coffees and no food.

Clive was direct with Evelyn and Claire. "When are you two going to tell Mr Mortimer that Louisa was in London for an interview for a large national paper? You can tell he's worried sick."

Both women glanced at each other. "I was about to tell him. Then you breezed in and things moved a little faster than I expected." She continued but never took her eyes of Clive. "I'll tell him this afternoon. Anyway, be honest, that doesn't account for her going missing does it," Evie retorted.

"No, I suppose it doesn't," Clive responded thoughtfully.

Evelyn looked at Clive. She weighed him up as being around forty to forty-five years of age, very fit, well-spoken and well-groomed. His dark features could be best described as a rugged handsome type of character. If you like that sort of thing, she pondered. "What do you really do for a living? You don't really capture my imagination that you're the head gardener."

Clive looked at her. "If you must know, I was in the Army for many years, intelligence service where I made major."

He continued, "We were in a false war when our whole section was attacked. Only two of us survived and a long story cut short, I left and I was in a dreadful state. Became homeless, lost my family, and drifted around for a couple years. Hit the meths and everything spiralled downhill from there. That is until one day, I was begging outside a main railway station in London when two women came up to me and offered me a job as a gardener.

"I was so confused. Here I am begging to fund cheap drink and these two old ladies, dressed in old fashion clothes, are offering me a job as a bloody gardener. I remember thinking how lovely they were. So unassuming and measured about my job offer. I looked at them and they said something like, 'It is a one-time job offer only'. So, for reasons I still don't fully understand, I got into a car with them. I don't think the driver was very impressed, having a smelly meth drinker in the car.

"But he said nothing. He dropped us all off at a big house in Kensington. Don't know where exactly. But it was a beautiful old place, both inside and outside. I went inside and a man showed me to a bedroom that had an ensuite shower room. He told me to get showered and put on the jogging pants, t-shirt, top and shoes. I could tell he was an ex-military type himself. He spoke in a way that you knew you were getting an order from him and not a request.

"I was right; he was the colonel. He had worked in the foreign office in the past as well as being in India before independence and fighting in Burma in the Second World War."

Clive spoke openly and honestly to the two young women, who listened intensely to every word he said. "I stayed in that house for about five weeks. I think I worked with various doctors and a psycho-therapist. All the stuff from the illegal war came out. The wife I left for my military career, blah de blah de blah. In the end, I arrived at the Manor. And you're wrong, I am the gardener! I have a great knack with plants.

"Learnt a lot from old Maurice. What a kind bloke he is! Has the patience of a saint. Rob, the other gardener, is also ex-services. He was with the special air regiment. He can speak lots of languages as well. We both realised that the Manor House, and its residents, are good people who rescued street people and people who have adverse childhoods from a lifestyle that they sometimes fall into.

"They knew we had skills that they needed. If they are to expose some of the bad things that are currently going on. They took a shine to you two, I can tell. They know your care backgrounds intimately. And trust me, they don't abide fools gladly."

"Where are they now?" Evie asked. "I had a notion they were going somewhere."

Clive smiled at Evelyn. "You're right. They went to Israel. They had to meet someone there and discuss getting someone's belongings back to them. Rob who speaks Arabic, Coptic and other languages is with them. I have to say this loud and clear that we are both very loyal to them. We know and appreciate that they saved our lives from the hellish miserable journey we were about to slip into.

"We are both very grateful to them. Rob was a captain who had a rosy career path in front of him. It goes to show anyone can fall into the dark side if pushed hard enough. They also have people in London and other cities that they have helped out, who are also very loyal to them, especially dutiful for making sure of the two Taylor women and the colonel's safety."

Clive then gave them a piece of advice. "I would like to suggest that you both get back to your working lives and when Lou shows up, leave it to her. She knew what she was getting herself into." At that point, he stood up.

Looking sharply at the two seated women, he said, "It's been nice meeting you two again, and I wish you both all the best for the future. Claire, stick with the job at the theatre. You have a great opportunity coming your way. Trust me. Ms Borowski, I'm sure our paths will cross again. I'll tell the ladies you both reached home safely and with the envelope, even though it was sealed by some miraculous intervention."

Claire looked bemused by these remarks but Evie never flinched. "Also, they will be so relieved to know I have the old film back in my hands."

At that point, Clive left the Shacks and climbed into a waiting taxi which he had strangely pre-ordered at this unknown pick-up point. They watched him drive away. He gave them a brief wave goodbye through the window and then he was gone clutching the steel briefcase.

They finished their coffees and were about to pay when the young waiter came strolling across. "The man paid when he walked out. He said the change belonged to you." He handed Evelyn the money which must have been around 40 pounds. "He said have a drink on him." Evie took the money and gave the young guy a fiver. "You have a drink on us as well." They both grinned at the gesture.

On the pavement outside, both women thanked each other for the last few days, deciding to meet up the following weekend and maybe catch a movie.

Strangely drink never appealed to either of these women to any great extent, but career success certainly did.

"By the way, where is the digitalised copy of the film?" Evie unexpectedly said.

Claire patted her bag, adding, "Safe and sound in my bag."

"Should I tell Mort?"

"I think you should but not until I can get it locked up in the basement. I think that all movies shown by the Theatre Festival group should be digitalised and a copy kept by Geoff for reference. The man from the basement. But very few people know that and we'll keep it that way for now."

Claire turned and walked towards her place of work, now wondering how the lovely Ms Rachael Cummins would treat her today. She should not have worried. Rachael was now away on the sick and Doug Collingwood, the long serving chairperson of the Old Deco Theatre, was sitting in the elegant Trustees' Chamber asking himself, "What does really happen on a daily basis in the Old Deco Theatre?"

He would find out over the next few weeks. *Thank goodness, Claire is back,* he thought.

Chapter X
Be Straight with Your Boss

The best way to find out if you can trust somebody,
is to trust them.

Earnest Hemmingway

It was now nearly 1.00 at the offices of the Evening Gazette. The office on the seventh floor, as was the custom, was now awash with the afternoon sunlight. Evelyn scrolled through her mobile messages and noticed that Stig had texted her to see if she had got back safely. Evie responded accordingly and thanked him for asking.

She was back at her desk, and Frank was opposite her and tapping methodically away at the old sit-up and beg typewriter like there was no tomorrow.

She took the laptop out of the draw, placed it on the desk and logged on to find 836 emails awaiting her on her new account. "How do you deal with all these emails?" Frank, and given the lack of any other person being present in the room, presumed that she was talking to him.

"I don't, funnily enough, you can call me old-fashioned, Ms Borowski, but people either phone me, visit me or write to me on pieces of paper. I don't even have an email address. I'm a great fan of George Orwell but he was a little premature with his assessment of 1984. Maybe he should have called it 2024."

He then continued, "And whilst Louisa Mortimer is missing in action, I am your supervising journalist. Right! So, I'm instructing you to delete all the emails that are on that Satanic machine before the date you started last week."

Evelyn looked at dear Mr Cousins for a moment. She smiled and did exactly what he ordered. Selected DELETE ALL and pressed with pleasure.

"Ms Borowski, I advise you start looking through old copies of the Evening Gazette and see how Lou approached her duties. The style she used and who she approached for articles of interest. You have Claire as a contact already. She seems a pretty smart cookie and in with the old crispy crafty arty crowd. This is basically your first week with the paper, so try and not get too involved and focused on one storyline.

"Also acquaint yourself with the paper's own Conduct of Journalism policy and associated protocols we have in place. And even more so, understand how it applies to your own everyday practice as a news reporter. Who incidentally deals with, if you haven't forgotten, with both people and their everyday sad and happy realities.

"And not as some would want you to believe as a neurotic student of journalism taught by psychotic lecturers? In fact, forget most of what you've learnt at university. Oh, by the way, congratulations and well done in obtaining a first. But now, you need to learn the survival techniques of a field journalist. You will undoubtedly need them in your crazy chosen career path."

With that, he looked up and said, "I am not to be disturbed for the next two hours. And you have a meeting with Mort in his office at 3.00 sharp. By the way, he's going away to London tomorrow. Something's bothering him about Louisa's disappearance. I never seen him like this before." Evelyn wasn't sure if he was speaking to her or himself.

Evelyn spoke, "Frank, one last thing. Can I discuss something quickly with you as my supervisor?"

He looked up. His craggy lined face and full head of greying hair looked reddish in tone as the afternoon rays of sunshine fell through the window. "If it's quick then."

"The one thing I never mentioned this morning was that Ms Taylor, the taller." He shook his head as to indicate that he hadn't a clue what she was on about.

"Frank, it's the name myself and Claire gave the two women. They are twins but one was tall and the other short."

"Ok, I get it," replied Frank.

"Well, somehow, she knew that Louisa was going to London for an interview with a big paper. I don't know if Mr Mortimer knew this or not. I'm assuming he doesn't."

"Well, you were right not to bring it up this morning but tell him straight away when you see him. Always be straight with your boss at all times, even if you don't like them. Obviously, you were distracted by the arrival of Bill and Ben at the meeting."

Evelyn broke in, "What did you think about Clive, the gardener?"

"No more a gardener than gormless Tommy out there. Ex-military I would expect. Your taxi driver said much the same thing to me. Remember, my advice is just be open and forthright with Mort. He can smell horse manure from five miles away. Now leave me alone, Ms Borowski, I need to finish my piece for tomorrow's early mid-day edition."

With that, Evelyn left the office and wandered through the indoor jungle maze to the stairwell and moments later, she was in Mort's office. A little earlier than planned, it has to be said.

"Please, take a seat, Evelyn." She did as she was instructed and sat down with her reporters' notebook on her lap.

"Well, again welcome to The Gazette."

"Mr Mortimer, before we start, I have something to report. I missed one vital observation out this morning. That is the Taylor twins knew for some reason that Louisa had gone to London for an interview with a large national. I did not want to say it this morning in front of the others. And then the arrival of Geoff and Clive interrupted proceedings a little."

Mort commented, "You sound more like a legal person sometimes."

Looking down at her notes on her knee, Evie retorted, "I do love courtroom dramas, especially *Rumpole of the Old Bailey*."

The editor responded with a chuckle and a rub of his chin. Then he returned to the matter in hand. "Thanks for telling me. Though I'm not surprised. She had for some time expressed a view that she would like to move on to a new challenge. Investigative Journalism for a large news channel was her dream. Working on stories where the underdog has no voice, women's rights, war refugees. That sort of thing."

Evelyn listened deeply as Mort's thoughts poured out.

"But that doesn't explain why she didn't come back to the North-East. And no contact, that's not like her. Did she say what paper?"

"No, I'm afraid not. Perhaps I should have asked Edith Taylor. But I really felt that if you prodded those people for too much information, they would close you out at this stage."

"You were probably right," Mort responded. "They are a strange crew, aren't they? But motivated to make a short documentary about something or another.

Well, that takes time, money and motivation, even for a fifteen-minute shortie. And how did Louisa get involved."

"Not sure. Remember, I only met her once when she interviewed me. I could have a word with Rachael if you like. Claire felt they were sort of friends."

"Only sort off!" Mort replied.

"What do you mean sort off?"

"Well, from what Claire described about the friendship thing is that it was obvious that Louisa kept in with her to find out what was going on in the theatre world. Rachael is a little flighty, very much into herself, and with little understanding about how the world really operates. People thought she had got the post because of connections and not ability. Even Ms Taylor, the taller, for some reason knew Rachael's background.

"In fact, they almost alluded to the detail that they had chosen this theatre for that very reason. The producer felt it would be easier to get their film shown at it. And because of the lack of management oversight; especially about what they should show at times."

Mort replied, "Makes sense, especially in the world of the crafty arty types. It's always who you know gets you the grants and funding. It's a shame, but it is what it is. And many good things can come out of that les affaire approach. Well, have a word with Claire but don't push it too far. She seems a good person. And you two obviously have hit it off."

"One other thing, Mr Mortimer. The film that was handed back to 'Clive, the gardener'. Apparently, it is the practice for the Old Deco Theatre to make a digital copy of all films in case they lose one or it is destroyed by fire or something."

"Right! So, who has the copy at the moment?"

"I believe, well in fact, I know the digital copy is in Claire's capable hands."

She then continued, "And nobody has seen the documentary yet. And the contents and subject matter is still under some form of legal restraint order that stops it from being shown, as the content could be interpreted as libellous."

"What about the article Louisa had drafted out and was supposed to read over with the two strange women before the showing of the film?" Mort asked.

"Well, I couldn't say for certain, but one fact is for sure. If Louisa had written a piece, an article as a follow-up, no one knows where it is."

"And the white A4 envelope? What's that about?" Mort asked.

"It was to be delivered to Louisa by hand. In fact, by my very own hands. I believe that the Manor Guesthouse crowd still believed that Louisa was still on board with them. Incidentally, they have left the country to attend a meeting in Israel. That's what Clive, the gardener, told us. Apparently, with the other member of the gardening crew in tow, his name was…"

Evelyn was looking at her notes. "Rob, that's his name. Who, if the story is right, is an ex-captain in some Special Forces regiment. Clive told me that Rob speaks many languages, including one called Coptic, whatever that is."

Mort retorted snidely, "Neither of those men are gardeners from what I been told. Clive moves with too much purpose to have been hanging around gardens pruning roses all his life. As you say ex-military and two people who could handle themselves." Evelyn thought that's about four different people who have come up with that same conclusion about the dear lovely gardeners, Clive and Rob.

Mort continued, "The envelope I've had put in the safe on the sixth floor. I'll make sure Louisa gets it."

Evelyn looked at Mort as he spoke openly and directly about when and what he wanted from her whilst an intern at the paper. She would be with the paper for at least six months, he told her.

"The paper had paid the bond on the flat, that was decided by Louisa; and for yourself, there was an allowance made available and you would receive it monthly as Louisa had instructed HR. In fact, Louisa had ensured you will be provided for whilst at The Gazette. Do you know we haven't had an intern for so many years? Louisa was in charge of arranging the internship. No one was just right."

Mort continued, "She sent me an email which said she was really impressed with you. In fact, whilst you were away, I dug out you HR file. Your CV and application were in it." Mort opened a buff-coloured file. "I see that you submitted a handwritten paper application. Why on earth did you do that in this day and age? You must have known that in most cases, it would work against you. Usually, if it's not an electronic version, no one even looks at it."

Mort looked over the desk at Evelyn. "You took a huge risk for some reason!"

It all went quiet for a while. Then Evelyn moved to the edge of the chair and leant forward. "All my life, I was brought up to believe and act as an honest and truthful person would. I worked twice as hard at uni than most other students.

But I'm certainly not looking for a sympathy vote, Mr Mortimer. I did it if you must know for my dead mam who fought so hard against her addiction.

"No, she wasn't in any way perfect but she tried so hard for me. And likewise for the lovely Lizzie, my guardian angel." For a moment, a deathly silence rained down on the room again. "So why did I complete this application in hand? For them I suppose. And yes, I used a stupid ruler to make faint pencil lines, and wrote with a fountain pen. Funnily enough, Ms Mortimer asked exactly the very same question."

Evie sat as she had done with Louise Mortimer the day she interviewed her, and before speaking to Lizzie. Once again, Evie found herself reflecting deeply, and in a spiritual way some would say. And simply so that she could find the simple logic to help her answer these complex questions she was being asked again.

She continued, "I truly believed and imagined that a prospective employer would see the honesty and the belief in myself, which ran through the words on the application form. As opposed to the majority of the people on my course that actually paid companies to apply for their jobs for them. I just can't believe that, but that's what it has come to. Lizzie truly believed, 'That someone, someday would appreciate my honesty that I put into creating a thought provoking application'.

"She said people can see that the world is becoming so false and deranged. And to answer your question, Mr Mortimer, I knew aversely in my heart that many short-sighted employers, whose desk my written application fell on, would immediately dispatch it to the bin. Well, my mam and Lizzie were proved right and here I am. In a job that I deserve. That's why I completed my application by hand.

"To test if the people I was taking all my skills, trust and hard work to were worth it. Were they worth giving my life to? Funny enough, Ms Mortimer said something like, 'The Gazette and me very much deserved each other than'."

Then after a few moments, Evie added, "She also said there is no room for passengers on the gravy train of work. I had to pull my weight or I'd be gone."

Mort smiled. "Oh, that sounds like my Louisa at her best."

"I promised her that I would not let her or the paper down. She even visited Lizzie and spoke to her about my possible internship and asked her how she felt about it, the move to Newcastle, my time in care and university. Louisa was so thorough but showed such care towards old Lizzie. And it has to be said very calculating about everything.

"She said she needed an assistant to help her with the increased workload in the future, and that she would cultivate me herself. Yes! Cultivate! That's what she said!"

Evelyn continued, "I'll say one thing, if she had arranged to see the Taylor women that Thursday afternoon in a local café, then the only reason she was not at that meeting is that something physically must have stopped her. And that thing was outside of her control I would suggest. That's the only conclusion I can come up with."

For about half an hour, Mort went over The Gazette's expectations of its staff. What leads she should pick up on and how Louisa styled her columns.

Evelyn, eventually, left Mort's glass bowl and was by now feeling extremely tired and fatigued. She returned to her office. Frank was already gone. It was noted that Frank left the office at 4.00 pm sharp most days and had done since time in memorial.

Evelyn turned off the desk light on Frank's desk and left the office. "I must speak to Lizzie tonight." In her mind, she knew Lizzie would want to know everything and every single detail about the weekend.

The No 1 bus came trundling down the road and stopped at the bus stop. Evelyn, still holding onto Stig's holdall, joined the fellow travellers on the bus and placed the bag onto the luggage rack. The journey home was luxuriously uneventful.

Back in the flat, there was a note. Stig was out for the night and wouldn't be back until the following evening. The note he left read, 'Hope all had gone well with the visit to NI. Meal in fridge and enjoy some telly; you must be knackered'.

She looked at her old Nokia phone, picked it up, and rang Lizzie. It was answered by a voice that had a rare softness in its tone and a temperament that hung onto every word that Evie spoke. Lizzie was the proudest person on this planet as she listened to all the events. No material reward in this world would come close to what Lizzie was listening to. Wanting detail after detail to be answered which made Evie smile.

She wanted to know what the pilot's name was. How many suits Maurice had? Was Clive from Viking descendants? Was there a lot of fog on the Tyne? Was Frank married? How was Lou and did she have a boyfriend? The inquisition went on for about an hour. Evie didn't have the heart to cut her off. She knew Lizzie would be soaking up every word as if she was living it.

She loved old Lizzie to bits, and so had her mam, and a type of love that cannot be replaced easily in this day and age.

Evie noticed that the sun was setting earlier over the park than it did a week ago. There were fewer people in the park now, but there was enough time for her to have a brisk walk before she ate the meal Stig had made her. *Strange, I've only known him for a week. It feels much longer.*

Chapter XI
A Surprise for Claire!

*It is easier to discover the truth from two lies
than discover the lies from two truths.*

Whilst Evie was having an eventful day at the paper, Claire's day was also about to take several unforeseeable twists and turns. After leaving Evelyn and Clive at the Shack, she ambled back to the theatre, fully expecting a real fun afternoon with dear Rachael, with her sly comments, innuendoes and patronising remarks. She passed underneath the Northern Guild of Goldsmith's art deco clock.

A large thing that has been suspended above the gild of goldsmith's shop entrance and hanging over the pavement since around 1932. Probably to remind the busy city folk what the time is and to remind them not to be late. The two black iron ornate large and small hands pointing at the circle of systemised Roman numerals said it was now 12.35.

She thought to herself, *Well, Mr Collingwood, you asked me to go with Evelyn*. At that point, her conscience started to question herself. *Why should I be really worried and to be exact worried about what? I am twenty-six years of age, soon to be twenty-seven*. Gained, no earned! Yes, earned a first-class honours degree. All be it one in Fine Arts and all the innuendoes that go with it.

She felt she had actually earned the first; even if the wider world has other views about Fine Arts degrees. After which she then had the core strength to follow her vocation in life, which had led her to be in this temporarily unpaid position. Where the hours she worked were long and, whatever way you looked at it, were seriously a joke.

At this point in her life and after spending the weekend with her newfound friend, Evie, who was a breath of fresh air to her dulling mind, Claire was clear with herself that if she was spoken to in a manner that was derogatory, sarcastic or be-little-ling, then her and her suitcase would be going straight home. She would look at other ways to advance her career in film and theatre production.

She had inherited a finite sum of money from her grandmother. Or to be more precise her adopted father's mother. Money that allowed her to follow her dream, as her gran had put it; although her parents firmly disagreed. This money would allow her to exist, no live, for around another six months. She still had time, loads of energy and motivation; a whole life in front of her.

Then at worst if it didn't work out, her committed to state school education parents would relish saying, "She now needed to get a proper job." And wouldn't they just love that! *Well, I'm a long way from being finished yet.*

As she walked along slowly dragging the suitcase behind her, she then thought about how she had only just met Evie. Not even a full week ago. Although, they came from very different backgrounds, how they had so much character and personality in common. Their lifetime interests in old cinema, especially the silent movies, the art deco buildings and the very early electric light theatres.

They talked about their own favourite actresses and heroines that had inspired them both in various ways. Recognising how these early actresses fought for their independence and own rights in a world dominated by men at the time. How these early women film stars found the inner strength to take control of their own lives and futures, but not in the current feminist form.

No! But in a more pragmatic, realistic style that needed a depth of character more aligned to both a saint and sinner. More of a way of fighting for equal rights rather than a takeover bid.

It was not long before Claire found herself standing on the pavement outside of the Art Deco Theatre and Cinema entrance, and still in deep thought about life. Given that the sky above Newcastle had clouded over, the low lighting from the Italian lamps from within the theatre pushed its way across the dirty pavement towards her. "To be or not to be…" Claire said under her breath.

She opened the door and pulled the small black suitcase inside with her. She was immediately met by Geoff from the basement, who had just been for a coffee with a group of theatre volunteers. She looked over to a table and there were about eight of them sitting with cups of coffee in front of them.

She noticed that they were all looking up at her as if all the heads had been tied together. All the volunteers simultaneously grinning whilst they raised their hands with a thumbs-up sign.

"What's going on, Geoff?" Claire asked at the same time smiling at the audience of volunteers and giving them a wave back like a mad woman would, then returning the thumbs-up salute. She wasn't sure why but she did it anyhow. She knew that these exceptionally talented volunteers were the soul and strength of this theatre and its life.

Even though modern management practices would have you believe everything could be worked out on a spreadsheet or pie chart. No, these people were the real deal and she had no doubts about that. They love the theatre scene that brings back to life a gone-by-time even if it was just a temporary thing. For her, it brought about so much happiness to so many for a short while.

Geoff answered, "You need to go to Rachael's old office. Mr Collingwood is there. He told everyone that when you arrive, you must go straight to his office."

"Any reason why?" Claire asked.

Geoff never answered but just scuttled away like he had a habit of doing when things were getting difficult or awkward. *Well, Miss Claire Smith*, she said to herself, *perhaps everything has been taken out of my hands about my future.*

Claire looked across the foyer and spoke, "Hello, Wendy, how's it going? All the shows and curtains up on time? Full house in all of them I hope."

Wendy Alexandria, who worked the ticket kiosk from 9-3, smiled back. "Everything is going well, Ms Claire. The ticket machines and internet ticket sales are all working for a change." She added, "It's nice to have you back. Hope you had a nice weekend." As always, Ms Wendy Alexandria had an infectious smile on her face.

She had been a volunteer for about ten years. The story goes that her aunt worked at the Art Deco in the wartime. She worked as an usherette and met her husband at one of the picture shows, apparently, when he was on leave from the Royal Navy. He was in the submarine service and everyone acknowledged how dangerous it was to be a submariner in wartime.

Leaving her with a smile, Claire moved away and climbed into the lift. She wouldn't have normally done this. Claire would always walk the stairs to see if all was in place and ship shape, but with the case and everything. In the lift, she got the distinct impression all was not well and something had taken place whilst she was away. She half expected bad news.

On the fourth floor, where situated the offices and store rooms, plus a small shop that sold keepsakes and coffees, she got out of the lift. Some of the offices accommodated the ever-growing insidious management strategies of the organisation. But the decor was still that of the original theatre from back in the early 1920s, very plush with walls half lined with lots of dark oak panelling.

The doors were stained in a dark wood colour and the original brass handles and finger plates shined for all they were worth against the dark background. The floor was still sparkling with the traditional Italian glass mosaic tiling. It would be over a hundred years old soon, but it looked as good as the day it was laid. Claire loved every single thing about the restoration of the building back to its glorious bygone days. A place the city should be so proud of.

She knocked on Rachael's door. No answer. At that moment, Mr Collingwood came out of the Trustees' Chambers and meeting room.

"Oh! Here you are, Claire. Got back safely then. Good."

At this, Mr Collingwood pushed the door open again and asked Claire to step inside. He wanted to talk to her about something.

They both stepped inside the chamber and sat down on two large Mackintosh styled chairs.

"Something's wrong, Mr Collingwood? What is it?"

"No. Not exactly wrong. It's Rachael; she's gone off sick and won't be returning for an extended period, probably months. Obviously, Ms Smith, everything discussed here is confidential and private and cannot be discussed with staff or volunteers. Do I have your assurances?"

"Completely," replied Claire.

"We've had a trustees' meeting this morning via Zoom or something like that." He then continued, "So we need someone to take over the reins as soon as possible. I've spoken to the volunteers this morning, restaurant staff and front of house staff."

He went on, "Apparently, they were quite clear and very direct that the place needs a new approach to the everyday running of the theatre." Mr Collingwood sighed a little. "I know this places you in a difficult position but the board, and more importantly its members, would like to offer you the position on an extended temporary basis.

"It's been agreed that I would come in three days a week to help you to take the theatre towards the original vision, as we saw it in the early days when the members, friends and volunteers took over the dilapidated building.

"You OK so far?" Doug asked in a quiet voice. "It's a lot to take in, but everything happened so fast after the fiasco that took place last Thursday." He took a sip of tea from an old mug as he searched for the next words.

"Also, I've had an interesting conversation this morning from an agent. In fact, a very influential and wealthy one may I add. A legal agent acting on behalf of a group of people who are members of something called the Entity Foundation."

Claire shook her head. "Never heard of them."

"Well, they certainly know you and Evie Borowski. In fact, they spoke very highly of you both."

"They did?" Her voice was full of surprise.

"They felt that you both conducted yourself most appropriately over the weekend just gone and would like to support the work of the theatre and support you in your career. I know this all sounds a little crazy but they are willing to pay for your internship for the next twelve months. But only in the position of acting theatre production manager."

"Is that not Rachael's title?"

"Well, yes and no. We changed the job description slightly so that you would work more closely with both paid and unpaid staff. You know that the restaurant is due to open at the end of this week and I've looked in. It's a nightmare to be honest." Doug was shaking his head slightly.

"Everyone seems to be in charge down there and very little is actually happening. I know it's a big ask. But can you take on this role at such short notice. It goes without saying I will be around to support you of course. The board feels between you and me and the gate post, Rachael had taken her eyes off the bigger picture a little bit.

"A bit more concerned with rhetoric than realism of the situation in hand. We have an opening to put together for Friday or we postpone it now. What do think?"

"It's all a bit fast." Claire sat a while thinking. But it was what she was born to do. She knew somehow this day would come if she kept her own working practices ethical. "Can you give me to the end of the day before I call that one?" She looked up. "I mean about the restaurant!"

Doug looked at her. "Of course, you can. And think about the job in your own time. And the opening. If you could let me know today sometime, I would really appreciate it.

"By the way, what happened at the weekend?" Doug asked.

"Not a lot really! But there was certainly something brewing in the background. Can I be honest, and this is not a pop-at-anyone. The group that had their documentary pulled at the last moment by the priest and his entourage, they were not too impressed by Rachael's handling of the situation on Thursday. And more so that she had not undertaken any form of compliance check on the movies been shown.

"Something we need to think about for the future when showing independent films from around the world and from diverse cultural backgrounds."

Doug retorted, "I'll make a list of things that need to be discussed further over the coming weeks. The board has two solicitors I know of. So why Rachael hadn't run some form of due diligence before trying to show them, I just don't understand it."

Mr Collingwood reached over and put his hand out. "Well, welcome onboard for now at least. I know the people around here will be very happy. They think very highly of you, along with your friends at the Manor Guesthouse. Do you know if Louisa has been in contact with Mort?"

"No, nothing. Mr Mortimer is really concerned. He's off to London tomorrow to try and find her, I think. I didn't really know her but apparently Rachael did."

"Well, I hope he does and quickly. It must be very worrying, your daughter going missing like that."

Claire looked at Mr Collingwood. "I'll get on the floor and get a grip on what's happening and what needs to be done. And maybe done quickly, I would suggest. I'll catch up with you through the day if that's OK, Mr Collingwood."

For the next few hours, Claire went through the building starting in the basement and the projectionist section. All movies for the week had been received from the distributor and next week's showings and beyond had been ordered. The ever-reliable Geoff was in complete charge of his dark empire and was on top of his game. Claire once again thanked him for the little job he had done for her regarding making a copy of the spool of film.

Claire went into the cafe area where three staff members were stood behind the counter.

Claire smiled and greeted them. "Hi, all. Jayne, Richard and Fern," she read their names out from their badges. "Who's been here the longest?" The new manager asked.

"I have," Richard responded.

"Well, Richard, I want to borrow one of your staff for the next day or two. Is that OK?"

"Yeah, sure," not really comprehending why she was asking him.

Claire looked at the two young women. "Who thinks they can read and write really well?"

Jayne was struggling with the question. Claire could see that.

Fern responded, "I done a level 1 course at college in administration. I hated it. Sitting in a classroom was so boring." Fern looked like a typical seventeen year old could look when discussing life in general.

"So why are you here, Fern?" Claire asked.

"Sent, I think, for job experience by the Universal Credit people. Blackmail really."

"Well, Fern, you will be with me for the rest of the day. When are you due to finish?"

"4.00."

"You got anywhere to go then?"

"Not really," said Fern with a puzzled expression on her face.

"Would you work late tonight?" By now, Fern looked confused. So many questions. Her personal assistant at Universal Credit said it would be easy. They got that wrong.

Claire asked again, "Yes or no. It's not a difficult question."

"Yes."

"Well, you're with me for the rest of the day."

Before leaving, Claire leant over to Richard. "I suggest you get all the tables cleared of dirty coffee cups and plates. Clean all the table tops down so they are ready for your next customers. Yes! Your next customers, Richard, as you're in charge now!"

Claire took Fern to Rachael's office on the fourth floor. Handed her a notepad and two pencils. "Just in case one breaks, hey."

Claire explained that she needs to follow her around and make a note whenever she indicated her to.

"Fern, I want you to help me make a list of things to do. The restaurant re-opens Friday, and it looks like we are not ready, and that means we are just a load of idiots playing at running a picture house. Well, we don't need that, do we?"

Claire looked at Fern for a response and, after a few seconds of silence, she said, "No, we don't!"

"That's the ticket, Fernie girl. Now we're a team!"

Claire moved about the building with ease, talking, smiling and when appropriate joking with the paid staff and volunteers alike.

On the third floor, Mark stood behind the miniature kiosk. His job was to welcome patrons and collect tickets when they arrived for the matinee of *Macbeth*. Mostly for school kids. An amateur production.

"Mark, the other night at the Independent Film Festival, you did the serving on the tables up here. You know the drinks and food. The tables were not covered with tablecloths. They were just bare. You know the expensive white linen tablecloths we have?" After a period of time that seemed an eternity, Claire emphasised, "Why not?"

Mark looked awkward and his eyes never engaged with Claire's face.

"Mark! Why not? You're not in trouble. I am. They should have been on the tables and I didn't check."

Mark looked up but never looked at her. "Well, Claire, they had not been returned. Rachael had lent them to someone and they were never returned." By now, Fern hovered around like a well-drilled secretary; the point of the pencil never more than an inch away from the lined notepad.

Claire turned towards her. "Get our white tablecloths back from!"

Fern being cute and very proper, said, "That's six words, Ms Claire."

Claire smiled happily in agreement, thought a moment and said, "Get our table clothes back; five words, I think. Glad you're keeping me right, Fernie girl. We don't have much time for great lists this week. But we need to start somewhere?" The rhetoric was not lost on the young Fern.

"Let's go back to Rachael's office to regroup, Fern."

"Ok." Fern asked in her seemingly nonchalant way, "Where is it?"

Chapter XII
And it Only Gets Better

*Never attribute to malice that which
is adequately explained by stupidity...*
                                Hanlon's Razor

After climbing the stairs for umpteen times, Claire and Fern found themselves outside of Rachael's office.

"Never been on this floor before. Rachael said I had no need to be."

Claire looked at her. "Neither have I really. I preferred working the floor. Wait a minute, Fern," Claire instructed. "Just stay here for a moment and take that pencil out of your mouth. You'll poison yourself."

Claire moved towards the Trustees' Chamber as it was signed posted on the thick old door. She knocked and Mr Collingwood's voice could be just heard from behind the door, "Come in."

Claire entered but not before indicating to Fern she should stay where she is and not wander off. Claire and Mr Collingwood spoke for about ten minutes. Claire gave him a quick appraisal of some of the staffing issues and how the volunteers were employed, or misemployed would be more correct.

Doug Collingwood for his part had been going through the income and expenditure, and certain correspondence. Correspondence he had not seen before which he found a little annoying. The funding streams that were ring fenced projects were a bit of a mystery to him too. Rachael had always reported the financial statement at the trustees' meetings. Everyone took her at face value, of course!

There had been management discussions over the years about bringing in a book keeper, but it had not moved past the talking stage. Rachael had spreadsheets that recorded expenditure and monitored the various milestones.

The board recognised that all these different jobs meant a lot of work for just one person.

Then Claire broached cautiously the subject of the restaurant that was due to be re-open on Friday.

"Mr Collingwood, today is Monday. I am going in to get an update and I would appreciate it if you could come in with me. I've only been in the restaurant area on one occasion. Rachael and the workers discussed progress but I was not privy to these talks."

Doug replied, "I must admit I've never been in there since it closed for refurbishment. We got a grant from the Warfield Trust who specialised in supporting architectural and art deco building restoration. This was alongside private donations."

Mr Doug Collingwood shuffled through a range of files and found the one titled 'Restaurant Restoration'.

"Let's go then," and they left the chamber together. Outside in the corridor, Fern was still rooted to the same spot.

Claire looked at Mr Collingwood. "I need to use Rachael's office if I am to undertake the role, even on a temporary basis. By the way, this is Fern. I found her lurking in the coffee shop. So, I borrowed her. She's a qualified admin worker and I would like her to assist me if that's alright."

The young Fern dressed in black trousers and shirt looked at Claire with a look that can only be called confusion. In fact, for a moment, she was wondering who Claire was actually talking about. Fern thought Level 1 in administration, from a college that basically gave her the certificate, hardly qualified her for the description Claire had so regally announced to Mr Collingwood, but she went along with it anyhow.

Fern quickly found Claire an interesting person who had a dry sense of humour, which Fern found amusing and it made her smile. Moreover, when Claire spoke, Fern actually found that she could understand what she was saying. Fern recognised that there was a very novel situation brewing today at work. Therefore, she would go along with everything, especially as it made the day less boring.

Mr Collingwood, Claire and Fern moved towards the restaurant. The doors still had the builder's protective plastic sheeting over them. Claire knew that this would not be an easy task. Theatre staff joked that Rachael believed that the contractors all had a crush on her. The facts from the file told Mr Collingwood quite clearly that they had numerous missed deadlines but always with the promise of making up the lost ground.

At the same time, Mr Collingwood realised that Rachael had approved milestone payments even though the work had not been completed. A very worrying situation for the theatre, he thought.

When the three walked in, they certainly were not ready for what met their eyes. The restaurant had been ripped apart but as for the updating and refurbishment, there were very little signs of any work being carried out.

As Claire and Mr Collingwood entered the restaurant, closely followed by Fern and her notepad and pencil, and who was by now enjoying her new job as chief recorder of list of to do things. And if truth be known, even more so when witnessing the squirming and wriggling of people that had not been challenged for a long time about doing absolutely nothing. Fern's pencil was now poised and in position for this one!

The three people were met by Marcus, a workman. "Hi, you shouldn't be in here without hard hats. We've spoken to Rachael about this and her responsibility to ensure the rule is obeyed."

"Well, Marcus, that's just the thing. Well, no, two things actually." Mr Collingwood's voice had taken on another tone and manner. "Rachael is no longer with us. And I must point out that it is the management board's responsibility to ensure the health and safety at work is adhered to. Secondly, I would suggest that little harm can come to us three from your pencil and paper as you sit there tackling the crossword."

All the time Doug spoke to Marcus, the girls knew the chairman's voice was loaded with a disguised malice.

Marcus who remained seated and that also annoyed Doug, already knew about the state of the refurbishment, or lack of it.

Doug asked directly, "Marcus, where are all your workers? You do know that this place re-opens on Friday and it looks to me like there is a hell of a lot of work to get done before that can happen."

Marcus spoke, "As my boss told Rachael, this place won't be finished for at least another three weeks at the earliest. We have other higher priority jobs to get on with."

"And when did your boss tell her this?" Even though very annoyed with the facts he was just being presented, Doug Collingwood's voice remained calm and precise.

"Last week I think," replied Marcus, who still had his pencil and paper in front of him. His face still covered with a smug smile which only added to Doug's worries.

"Do you have your boss' number, Marcus? I think I need to cancel the contract immediately before more precious funding is wasted."

The worker quickly forwarded Mr Collingwood his boss' number, saying, "He'll only tell you what I've told you."

Doug Collingwood never removed his glare from the worker's face for one minute. Then immediately pressed re-dial. Then spoke very bluntly to his boss about terminating the contract with immediate effect; and that he will be receiving a letter from the theatre's legal department by tomorrow.

A letter including the subject about the payments for work not carried out and the many missed legal milestones. He closed down the conversation by ending the call. Marcus' face was a picture and the smug grin had now completely disappeared.

"Well, one thing, Marcus, you can be sure of is that you and your company will not be finishing the refurbishment of this beautiful restaurant. You can take that one to the bank as they say!"

Doug looked at Fern. "Can you please escort this person off the premises, Miss Fern?"

"No problem, Mr Collingwood Sir," Fern replied whilst removing Marcus' hard hat from the table and handing it to him before holding the door ajar.

"I need a black coffee!" Doug said as he walked silently out of the war zoned restaurant and returned to the Trustees' Chamber. Doug knew he had various priority phone calls to make. About twenty minutes later, Doug Collingwood entered Claire's temporary office. No, let's be kind, Claire's new office. Doug nodded at the women.

"Fern, Claire, I now feel a little more composed. So can we go back into the restaurant and try to come up with a short-term plan of some kind." Claire and Fern glanced at each other. Whilst Doug was informing various people of the situation, they had been trying to track down the missing tablecloths and find the various members of staff's contact details. Claire had spoken to the restaurant manager who was due back from holidays on Wednesday.

He believed that the tablecloths were still at an art gallery on the other side of the river. Claire looked up at the clock. It was 4.45. Looking at Fern, she said, "Aren't you supposed to be finished by now?"

"Miss Claire, you told me to stay until I could go. Anyhow you said we are a team," Fern said that with a smile coming across her face that Claire would become so used to as time went on.

Mr Collingwood asked Claire to join him in the Trustees' Chamber.

Claire, before leaving the office, turned to her new young assistant, "Fern, you trace down those very expensive tablecloths." Turning to Mr Collingwood, "I think we need a staff meeting so we can update everyone on the progress."

"I would totally agree," he replied.

Mr Collingwood looked at the young girl, Fern, who looked completely at home at the small desk in the corner. "Press 9 for an outside line. And, Fern afterwards can you go down and get us all a cup of coffee or tea? Bring it to the restaurant and wait for us there." At that, Claire handed Fern the restaurant keys. "And don't let anyone else in. OK."

In the chamber, Doug shared with Claire that it all started that morning at around 8.00 with a phone call from Rachael's mum. "Apparently, Rachael felt under a lot of stress and taking away her assistant for the weekend had just added to her complications and she felt undermined." Doug replaced the word complications with insecurities in his thoughts but remained guarded.

Doug explained that Rachael's mother, Martha, also reported that she has a sick note for two months. In all honesty, Martha shared with him that they feel Rachael would prefer another type of career. "Doug between you and I, the poor girl wasn't coping too well," said her mum. Doug had taken the hint, listened and behaved impeccably on the phone to Martha, who was also a long-time friend of Doug and his wife.

He knew as he listened that the day was going to be a very difficult one, but how difficult was yet to be understood. Although, he did feel that this would give him the chance to get amongst the day-to-day stuff, then to assess what needs to happen to the prestigious theatre and cinema known locally and lovingly as the Old Art Deco.

By the end of the long telephone call, Mr Collingwood and Rachael's mum had come to an agreement that she didn't need a sick note and that she would be paid two months' severance. Doug wished her well for the future.

Without sharing anything with anyone, and some tough eight hours later, he was so glad that Claire was back from Ireland. As the intern, she had clearly taken a deep interest in the theatre's day to day running and history. He had heard many good things about her from staff and volunteers alike. Apparently, she got on well with most people. Was always customer-focused and loved the Old Art Deco, and was a great hands-on organiser and could evidently multi-task.

After Doug had come off the phone to the company's solicitor, who supported Doug's actions 100%, he made his way back to the restaurant. Doug was met by Claire who was busy talking on her mobile phone to Richard, the restaurant manager, getting a catch-up about staffing arrangements, and what had been agree with staff and VIPs, for the re-opening. Claire had always felt that Richard was a reliable person.

He spoke with a voice of authority that gave you confidence. He had been working in the restaurant for about eight years, starting as a chef and then the manager. He could work both front of the house and kitchen when needed. He explained on the phone to Claire that he told Rachael that things were just not happening.

He felt Racheal just didn't want to listen and he agreed to pop in the next day even though he was not due back into Wednesday. Things needed sorting out one way or the other, he said to Claire on the phone.

Claire noticed immediately that Doug looked uncomfortable as he explained that he had basically cancelled the contract. "They were just having a laugh at our expense. And I hate to say this, we paid 60% upfront for basically nothing."

He continued, "We also have five paid staff and an opening night that we have to cancel." Claire got the feeling that Doug was taking things a little personally now which was understandable. At that moment, Fern walked in the door with a tray of coffees. Richard, the coffee shop kid, had also added some scones and jam. Fern placed them on the table where the smug builder once sat doing his crossword.

"Well, Claire, I think we need to cancel the opening night. And let people know that it will have to be delayed indefinitely due to unforeseen building circumstances."

Claire looked around the room which resembled a building site and a sinking feeling came over her too.

Mr Collingwood looked directly at Fern. "Did they ask you in the coffee shop what was happening up here?"

"Yes, they did."

"And what else…"

"Nothing else. I told them that you would tell them something when you had something to tell and it's not my job to say."

Mr Douglas Collingwood smiled for the first time today. "Well done, young lady."

They all sat pondering and discussing the future of the beautiful Art Deco Restaurant and the old smoking room next door.

Fern with pencil and notebook at the ready, whilst Claire added milk and sugar to the coffees. Mr Collingwood was now sitting on an old seat, cross legged, and his left hand rubbing his temple. They drank and ate the scones in silence.

It was now well past 6.00. Suddenly, the door opened and a small stocky man walked in. "Hello, Uncle Maurice," said Fern.

Maurice looked at the three. "Oh, lass, what have you been doing. You're not in trouble again with that mouth of yours?"

"Who are you?" Mr Collingwood asked.

"I'm her uncle, Maurice Woodman. Fern lives with me and Doris, the wife, and has done so since she was eight years of age."

Doug cut in. "Well, may I say, she has been the most helpful young lady one could have asked for today, and you must be very proud of her."

Claire added, "Yes, she is excellent at list making and tracking down missing property, and has provided us with coffee in times of great stress. She has kept me right on many things today." Claire smiled at Fern who was fidgeting a little as she was embarrassed with the praise being heaped upon her.

A stranger could tell Uncle Maurice was also gobsmacked by his silence. He had automatically presumed she was getting her cards again.

Doug lent over. "Would you like a cup of coffee? Fern get your uncle a cup and saucer." Maurice was waiting for the punch line. He had a surprised expression on his face as Fern moved towards the door and left, without any grief or sarcastic comments been exchanged.

Doug looked at Maurice who must have been in his mid-sixties. "Yes, she's been a great help today." Maurice still could not believe they were talking about his niece, Fern, who even some of the worst chavs in the neighbourhood would give a wide birth to.

Maurice looked about the place and asked what happened here.

Doug thought, so what? Just tell him. He explained to Maurice, a complete stranger except for the fact he was a person who had a duty of care for one of his current staff members, what had happened that very day. Two complete strangers discussing the problem of the building site.

Maurice and Doug spoke for what seemed to be hours. It was now past 7.00. They lifted boxes together, moved things about a bit. Maurice explained to Doug that lots of builders now have a number of jobs going alongside each other. Saying, "Then at the same time, they often find themselves over-committed and things fall behind on all the jobs. Builders often as not, string out the customer with tales of poor supply chains who have in turn let them down."

Maurice then explained to Doug how he had worked in the local shipyards as a senior fitter, working on many of the great ships that had sailed from the Tyne. By trade, he was a master carpenter and foreman before the shipyard closed. He and Doug looked at some of the butchered wood panelling and the half-connected electrical wiring.

"This is a disgrace," Maurice said running his hands over the oak panelling. "It's a wonder the Heritage people have not been involved. Given this building must be Grade II listed status."

Doug could tell the Maurice knew what he was talking about. "Real oak and cherry panels are the originals," said Fern's uncle. The old glass tear-dropped chandeliers that had twelve arms each had been banged around and little care had been taken to protect them.

The kitchen at the side had been stripped of the old equipment and the stainless-steel benches removed. At a glance, Maurice felt that given the number of cardboard boxes stacked up, the new kitchen to be fitted was all there.

As Doug and Maurice moved about the restaurant, the two young women picked up old cardboard and rubbish and placing it into black bin bags, continued to tidy up. Why they did this, the women were not sure but they felt Doug and Maurice needed space.

"When you opening, Doug?" Fern was surprised when her uncle called Mr Collingwood by his Christian name, but it's been a funny day all round, she thought.

"Was to be Friday," replied Doug.

"Well, I would be glad to help out if you would let me."

"Well, we can always use volunteers to help out." Doug offered his hand. "Welcome onboard the sinking ship."

"Maybe not," the shipyard worker answered. At this point, Maurice walked over to a corner and made a number of phone calls on his not so modern mobile.

"Well, I've spoken to my old dockyard mates and they are quite up for putting this place together again. But we would have to start early tomorrow morning. And I mean early! Funny enough, and you may not believe this, Doug, but the crew who were here have done most of the hard work. But they should have been more careful with the furnishings already in place.

"Believe it or not, most of the cruise ships that left the Tyne would have had fittings like these in their officer's cabins, public areas, and ballrooms. All for the first class, of course."

Doug looked at Maurice. "Are you kidding me? You could have this place put together for Friday. Four days?"

"Well, we could give it our best shot."

Fern, who was standing listening to the conversation, felt so proud that her uncle was being valued for his carpentry skills once again. She knew how hurt the workers were when they were laid off out of the blue, so that the ship-building industry could be slowly moved to the far east.

Doug listened intently to her Uncle Maurice. A proud man, who after a lifetime of working as a ship's carpenter and gaffer, was made redundant and without any real warning. His next job was collecting up the supermarket trolleys. This had made him very sad, insular and bitter. He was a man who, along with his mates, had built the great liners from raw materials from the ground upwards and fitted them out in beautiful exotic woods from around the world.

He had made various ship's captain's chairs from the trunks of rare trees. French polished table tops until they looked like mirrors.

Doug and Maurice went back to the chamber on the fourth floor but before leaving, instructed Claire, "Can you and Fern secure this place please."

At the door and before leaving the restaurant, Doug pointed towards the large exit door at the end of the passage that led to the toilets. "Maurice, can you use the exit to come and go, as the rest of the theatre will continue to operate tomorrow. At the end of the fire stairs, you will find a large skip which is ours. Although other people keep throwing their junk in it, I noticed."

Claire and Fern walked back up the stairs and entered the chamber. Doug and Maurice were pouring over the architect's drawing. Maurice was tracing things out with his stubby fingers attached to his strong scarred workman's hands. Pointing and running his fingers over architectural drawings, that showed a large stamp saying 'Approved' on them with a date.

"As I thought, the architect has not altered any of the original building design. This always alarms National Heritage if you do. Everything is basically an upgrade or a replacement.

"Well, Doug, I'll be here at 4.00 prompt and you'll have the exit doors opened for us. There will be five of us all together. My gang from the shipyards. I tell you, Doug, they'll be buzzing tonight. Most still have their wives and they will be putting up their sandwiches and flasks right now. Just like the old days."

Maurice continued, "Mr Collingwood, stop looking so worried. You now have the A team of shipyard fitters on the theatre's side. I know a sparky that will drop everything for me and test the electrics tomorrow morning. I'll get the lads set on their tasks. But they'll know what needs to be done."

With that, Maurice and Fern left but not before Fern asked Claire what time does she want her in tomorrow. This question surprised Maurice.

"Well, Fernie, I'll be in at the same time as Mr Collingwood. We all have a lot of hard work to do if we are to get the restaurant opened by Friday, and operating, even if it is a slim chance, we must give it a go."

Fern smiled. "I'll be in with my uncle then. We all have a lot to do."

Claire and Doug remained for about another half an hour discussing everything and nothing, then both went their own ways.

"Well, it can only get better," said Mr Collingwood to Claire with a warm smile and adding, "It's all in the hands of the gods now! Good night."

Chapter XIII
Thank Goodness for the Workers

The darker the night
the brighter the stars are.

Fyodor Dostoevsky

As agreed, the evening before, and no truer to their word, eight people stood in the centre of the old tea rooms the next morning, soon to be re-named the new Art Deco Theatre restaurant. It was exactly 4.00. It was still dark outside and the exit door was wide open to the outside world. At that very moment, a middle-aged woman with a cheeky grin entered through the exit door carrying a large toolbox and joined the good people inside.

Maurice looked at her. "Hi, Helen, you didn't need to be here this early." Helen, a renowned electrician from the estate, and who was Trevor, the plumber's daughter, had volunteered to help out as soon as her dad told her about the mad situation, regarding the old theatre refurbishment and its possible delay.

"The way I see it, you need the electrics up and tested by 12.00. And if you are going to refit the kitchen area today, an early start is just what is needed," replied the hefty woman with a no-nonsense voice. "And anyway, Maurice, the club and community centre are buzzing with pride that you were asked to help out the old theatre and get it up and running." Helen ended the conversation by saying, "Maurice, where are the schematics for the electrics?" And the request meant now.

"In the brown folder on the table, Helen, marked electrics." Maurice looked at her and thought what a gem. Helen, for her part, took the diagram and moved towards the kitchen area. She knew fitting a restaurant kitchen would need extra breakers and the like and started to chase down the distribution and fuse boxes.

Maurice moved a large piece of paper from the file he had. The paper had a strange diagram all over it with different plumbing instructions on it and handed it to the plumbers. "Thank you, Maurice, yes, that's ours," said Trevor, the time served plumber. "...the designers would have thought of everything regarding the plumbing."

Trevor, Helen's dad, took the design instructions and puzzled over them for a moment, whilst his mate brought in more toolboxes and various lengths of copper and plastic piping.

At that moment, Richard from the coffee shop appeared through the exit door like a bolt of lightning, startling the group for a moment. "Morning, I thought you guys would like coffee and tea to keep you going. So yes, I'm here to help Claire."

Claire shook her head. "Thanks, Richard, but how did you know?"

"Fern phoned me and said it's all hands to the pumps, whatever that means," he added. The older men grinned at both him and his lack of understanding to the meaning behind the saying, but with a large amount of appreciation in their faces for his sentiments and the offer of coffee.

All the older men were wearing old-fashioned overalls with straps that came over the shoulders which joined a flap at the front with a strange button affair for holding them together. One had blue, two had brown and two had white sets of workers' overalls. Doug passed them a box of hard hats and instructed them to wear them at all times.

He also handed Richard one for when he was in the building site area. Richard took hold of it and felt he was now part of a strange team. Something that was lacking before, he thought. It seemed to him that staff just come and go as they please. He didn't even know the names of most of them.

Maurice was gazing down at the drawings of the refurbishment directed the men to their tasks. All the time the tradesmen pointed out possible problems and then together reached agreements with him on the best way around them. Doug was so impressed with the way they spoke and listened to each other's problems. Total respect for each other's work was so evident.

One thing they all agreed with was that they did not have time to do things twice. By 4.25, the various trades moved off to their allocated tasks in a quiet and efficient manner.

Helen poked her head through the large serving counter and said, "The power for the ovens was ready to connect and that the fuse box had been tested, so everything was sweet to go OK. You can also use the points for power tools."

The plumbers started to chase the water pipes and stop cocks and tap connections as they had so many times before.

Maurice turned to Doug and said, "By dinner time, I'll probably have a list of items that we need. Will that be alright?"

"Of course," Doug replied.

"And one other thing, Doug, can you send Claire and Fern to pick them up. Fern knows the suppliers and she'll not let anyone short change you."

"No, that's fine," he said turning to Claire who agreed in an instant.

Claire turned to Fern. You stay here and, as your uncle finds the bits and pieces, he needs you to make a list and write them down. OK.

Fern laughed thinking is there any type of list other than one written down before replying, "Ok, and in less than six words." At the same time, Fern waved her pencil and the notebook in her hands. Adding, "Richard has asked me what we have to call you?"

"Claire will do. It's my name! Is that six words?" She added and both women grinned at the mischievous joke.

As Claire and Mr Collingwood were leaving, Richard returned with a tray of teas and coffees and placed them on a table with some biscuits and toasted rolls.

Maurice, with his charm, made the point, "Thanks, son. You know they can all work, eat and drink tea at the same time."

The older men laughed and a voice in the crowd was heard to say, "Some things never change, do they, Maurice."

He smiled back at them with that gaffer's look and said, "Get it done!"

The men repeated the words "Get it done!" like a mantra which they all laughed at.

Claire and Mr Collingwood promptly returned to the chambers and discussed what to do next. Claire was adamant that they meet the day staff and have at least ten minutes with them in the coffee shop and explain to them what the plan is for the restaurant. She and Doug knew that if they didn't have a meeting, then the rumours would be rife. And rumours only spread discontentment, and this week in particular, they really did not need negative feelings in the Old Deco Theatre.

Later that morning, Claire and Doug both went back to the building site and helped unpack the kitchen equipment and steel worktops from the packaging and placed all of the waste in the skip outside. On the tables at one end, Maurice and another man, and Richard of course, laid out the kitchen equipment against the drawings.

Trevor, the plumber, shouted through that the water is on and the couplings ready to be connected to the sinks, dishwashers and steamers. Maurice took the pencil from behind his ear and under his cap and shouted, "Very good," and ticked off the jobs on the list with his sharp pencil.

Over at the Gazette, Evie was already at work in the office on the seventh floor. She now felt that she shared the office with some equity with Mr Frank Cousins, although she accepted he was her temporary supervisor. She learnt that being in early had always allowed her to get a good start. Yesterday had gone so quickly and she knew from the text she received from Claire that something had changed remarkably at the Art Deco for her newfound friend.

It was agreed yesterday, Monday, that Evelyn should have a week's settling in time and by then, Lou may have reappeared into the land of the living. Mort had left for London early that same morning and was already on his way. Lou had been missing for over a week now. He was going to visit some old contacts to see which paper his daughter had an interview with.

In the morning, Frank had come in early too, to get ahead of the game as he put it. His telephone rang continuously from 07.30 for about an hour. His old contacts and racing muckers passed him information from the tracks around the country.

"Morning, Ms Borowski, and how are you today?"

"Getting there I think, Mr Cousins. Lou had left me some emails about what events that are taking place in the North between now and Christmas. Moreover, the pantomime season had been announced and who and what was being staged." She was going to put together a short piece about what was on and what was coming to the area.

Evelyn was going to pull it together today. She visualised five hundred words that would fill the two columns that were situated between the many adverts that promoted what events were on around the toon.

"She asked me to draft a piece for her to look at. I've checked her columns for the last year as you said. And she does have a specific Orwellian style she uses. From the outside, she tries to keep the readers interested, the sentences short and plain and gives them short stories that are emotionally humorous."

Looking towards Frank, she asked, "How's Mr Mortimer?"

Frank looked up. "Well, and if I'm honest, I don't think he's too good. He texted me before he boarded the flight to London this morning. It's a queer one that! Louisa taking off like that. Without a word. She's been a bit mad in the past when she was younger, but I thought she got over that. It must have been a bit of a kick to hear she was attending a job interview."

Evelyn looked out of the window across the city skyline deliberating what to say. "I don't think it did actually. He seemed to have half expected it. That's what I felt."

At that moment, Evelyn's phone rang on the desk. It was Claire.

"Hi ya. Did you get my texts? It was mad here yesterday afternoon when I got back. I think I'm the new manager. But of what I'm not sure." She started to relate the previous afternoon and evenings proceedings.

"Can I stop you for a minute? Mr Cousins, as my supervisor would you listen to what Claire, the manager of the Old Art Deco Theatre, apparently has to say." Evelyn put her on speaker and Claire quietly relayed what had happened and the events around the restaurant refurbishment. How a group of local Gordie men and women had stepped in to save the day. Claire then ended the call as she had to be somewhere else, a staff meeting or something like that.

Frank looked at Evelyn and then spoke, "It sounds like a nice story is brewing. And we all need them occasionally. I want you to take gormless Tommy over to the theatre and get some good pics of the before and after saga. Get a bit of a background to what led up to the events, etc. But leave old staff out of it. Keep it positive. Upbeat you know what I mean."

Frank stopped for a moment and after pondering the situation continued to speak. "In fact, I would suggest you hang around there with Claire for a while and get a feel of the old theatre and what it means to the members and public alike."

Frank continued, "The piece for Thursday's edition, write on your laptop from the downstairs cafe at the theatre. You'll find all the boujee types there bashing away at something that is so important, at least to their selves. And give yourself time to look out of the window to see how the city moves. How it breathes. What's important to it and its people? Talk to the laid-off workers and what it means to do something meaningful in their lives again.

"Pull a community interest story together. A nice one, mind you. Mort and Doug go back a long way and have always been really good friends. Very supportive of each other, even in the bad old days. Make it secretly evocative but emotionally uplifting, Ms Borowski. Like Lou would have…"

Evelyn checked with Claire before setting off to make sure the people involved would be up for a piece in the community section of the Newcastle

Evening Gazette, including the opening night. Claire quickly checked with Doug who agreed. "A bit of good news would be just the ticket, Frank, pardon my pun, and what the Old Art Deco Theatre may need at the moment. Ticket sales are dwindling," Doug said with a little concern in his voice.

Before you knew it Evelyn and Tommy stepped into the theatre foyer. By now, it was a little after 11 am. September had arrived without any announcement. She had to wait for Tommy to get his act together. Evelyn now understood why maybe Frank gave him the odd nickname he did but she would keep an open mind.

The cleaner who was mopping the Italian tiles in the foyer said, "Please mind the wet tiles," in her vigorous broad Gordie voice, at the same time pointing to the danger sign.

"Where is Claire?" Evie asked.

"She'll either be in the restaurant or in her office, Hinny," came the reply. The woman turned her back on Evie and continued to mop the mosaic floor.

"Her office?" Evie smiled to herself; she was right. *She was going to be in charge one day of the running of a theatre. But not just as quick as people would have expected it, I bet.*

The journalist and photographer stopped outside the restaurant doors. "Shall we have a look inside?" Tommy said. Without hesitation, Evelyn responded by pulling open the door. The two people were shocked with what they saw. The whole room seemed to be a hive of activity. Fern approached them. "I'm afraid this is a hard hat area by order of Mr Mortimer and Ms Claire."

"Where is Ms Claire?" Evelyn asked.

Fern, now in white painter's overalls and holding a paint roller in her hand, replied, "In her office on the fourth floor. Just follow the stairs up and turn right at the top and walk along the panelled corridor. It has Rachael on the door, though it won't be Rachael inside, it will be Claire." Evelyn looked at Fern and thought about the way she recited everything in a low monotoned voice, especially the amount of detail she shared. Perhaps she will make a good reporter one day.

Evelyn knocked on the door with the name Rachael on it. "Hello, come in," the recognisable voice said from the inside. Both Evie and Tommy entered and there was Claire. She seemed a little more buoyant in herself today, thought Evie. In fact, a lot more buoyant. Claire caught her up on all the gossip, changes and most strangely the 'promotion', although only temporarily.

For Claire herself, a temporary operations manager role at the Old Art Deco was enough for her at present. She brimmed with pride and knew that she would make it her own. The doubts she held about herself at times had now all dissipated into the atmosphere. Her own theatre of dreams was now around the corner. She could not wait to tell her parents the excellent news but probably for all the wrong reasons.

She explained to Evie how Mr Collingwood had addressed the day and split shift staff, announcing that Rachael had decided to move on, and from now on, Claire would be taking over her duties. The staff had all clapped and congratulated Claire on her promotion. She told Evie how Fern's family and friends had come to the rescue of the theatre, and how they started the refurbishment work on the new Art Deco Restaurant immediately.

"They had all come in at 4.00 that morning and had set straight to work. They are all ex-shipyard workers and their families you know."

Evie replied, "Well, Claire, me and Tommy are here to do a piece for the Gazette about these heroes you found from the community. Who would think that a group of retired working-class people coming to the rescue of the good name of the Old Art Deco Theatre and Cinema?"

At that moment, Fern walked in draped in her well-used baggy painter's overalls. "I have a list of things Uncle Maurice needs for the restaurant area." Claire introduced her to the people from the Evening Gazette. "Meet my new assistant and all-around know-it-all, Miss Fern, or Fernie to her new friends. And to be fair, without her insight, none of this would have been happening."

"OK less of the drama stuff, Ms Manager. Uncle Maurice needs these bits and pieces ASAP. And he said ASAP." At the same time Fern removed the white painter's overalls and placed them on the back of the chair by the desk in the corner.

Evelyn and Tommy agreed to float around and get as many before and after shots as they could. "That is without getting in anyone's way," Claire added. Evie agreed that she would speak to the volunteers and workers in the building site before taking any photographs.

Fern was ready and Claire had her car keys in her hands. They left the building via the fire exit but not before checking that Maurice had nothing else to add to the perfect list. Maurice automatically handed Claire a sheet of polythene to cover her back seat and boot. "The parts we required were only small items but it's best to keep your car clean pet," he said with a helpful voice.

The two women left by the exit. Clair had the debit card in her bag that allowed her access to the ringed fenced bank account for the refurbishment. Fern had the list. She had to admit that Rachael had the financial management all in hand. It was a pity that she could not put it into practice the good recording when actually dealing with suppliers and contractors.

It looked like she had taken their word at all times on face value and never checked the completed work or orders for herself.

Within fifteen minutes or so, Claire's car pulled into the car park of Austin's plumbing centre. They walked in and she noticed Fern was in automatic mode. She grabbed the large catalogue and started writing out the parts numbers on the printed orders list form. She flicked through the pages like a professional trades person. At times having a conversation with herself, comparing and contrasting prices, and making a decision by noting the form.

Claire just looked in amazement. "How do you do that?" She asked with a quizzical look on her face.

Fern, who never took her eyes of the task in hand, answered, "I used to do it all the time for Uncle Maurice. I was supposed to be at school but that was a waste of time, so I bunked off. Uncle Maurice got angry, so did the social workers, so did the youth justice people, so did the teachers, so did the court people, so did everyone else, except my mum and her lousy boyfriend; they certainly didn't give a dam.

"But no one could explain to me what it was all about, and certainly no one listened to what I wanted with my life. So, I ended up most days with Uncle Maurice, my mum's oldest brother, as his unpaid apprentice and stores person extraordinaire. If they needed it and it was out there, I could source it. I was really good at it."

Fern continued to multi-task and speak, "So they sent me on an idiot's course in administration level 1. They don't have a clue, do they? I mean how they can end a young person's will to live should be bottled and sold?"

It was the most Claire had heard Fern say in the last twenty-four hour period about herself. She walked over to the trades counter and handed the completed order slip to the man at the counter.

"Well, look who it is? Haven't seen you for a long time, you little pest," the man behind the counter said. He continued talking to other staff. "Ya knows, this one does not miss a thing. She was taught by the best in the business, our

Maurice." He smiled. Claire understood that he was paying Fern a backhanded compliment but she felt that Fern did not recognise it as such.

Fern's robotic response was, "Just get me the order together and don't miss out anything. This is my boss and she does not want to trape down here twice in one day for your mistakes ye know." At all times, Fern kept the power but Claire could see she did not see it.

The man laughed and shook his head. "I see you haven't changed, full of charm as always."

"As quick as you can, we have a deadline to meet."

Claire thought, *You have to hand it to her, she was a woman not to mess with*.

Within thirty minutes, they were back at the building site. "Here's all the things, Uncle Maurice."

"All of it?" Maurice checked.

"Well, I wouldn't have said 'all of it' if something was missing, would I?"

Maurice shook his head and smiled. Fern was not one for many words, but the words she used were plain and cut to the chase. The workmen came over to the two boxes of fittings and parts. Maurice sternly reminded them not to lift something if it's not yours. If it is yours, take it and keep it safe within your workspace. No time for second trips today.

The Old Art Deco Theatre settled down that afternoon to a much quieter pace. Outside the building site, soon to be the new restaurant, the scheduled films continued to be shown on time and live theatre carried on as nothing else mattered in the world. Except today, there was a little more background noise. The coffee shop filled, emptied and filled up again with punters from the surreal city centre.

Richard and his assistant continuously providing an endless stream of exotically named overpriced coffees with strange ingredients; with coffee beans sourced from unknown places from around the globe. Danish pastries, cakes and glamorous freshly made sandwiches were all available, and of course, the icing on the cake for an ultra-modern café. A good assortment of vegan and vegetarian choices for the up and coming city workers to scoff away at like a human machine of munching red and black ants.

Claire and Fern remained in the restaurant area to help out with the work. They both had long handled rollers and were painting the ceiling with a coat of satin white paint. But of course, as always, under the close eye of Uncle Maurice, who insisted that all areas were protected correctly with dust sheets and they had to be the right thickness as he wanted to protect the expensive royal red and black tartan carpet that covered the whole seating area.

The two women moved along swiftly, Fern painting in one direction and Claire following in the opposite behind her, so as to ensure a good covering and finish.

At around 6.00, Richard walked in with a tray of sandwiches, teas and coffees. In the sandwiches were cheese and ham. Earlier in the day, he had tried the workmen with a range of the more exotic sandwiches but noticed, although gratefully received, they were not touched. The cheese and ham ones were devoured with the speed he hadn't noticed before in his customers in the coffee shop downstairs.

Claire asked him how he had managed today with only one assistant. It was better actually as we were kept busy and Joanna, his assistant, really stepped up to the mark today. The sandwiches were brought in from outside. This helped cut out the preparation time but Richard, the coffee kid, said he'll be happy when Richard, the chef, and the kitchens are up and running; and we can source all food to customers from within the business itself.

In all her short time at the Old Art Deco, she had never heard Richard give any form of perspective of how it should be run.

"Richard, get yourself home, you've been here since 4.00. But we will carry on your conversation next week when things begin to get back to normal. If you have any other good ideas for the coffee shop, pass them to Fern who will make a list. Make sure your ideas are no longer than six words or there could be trouble." The young Fern gave a sarcastic grin to her new boss. In fact, her first boss.

By 7.30, the ceiling had been painted; the oak panelling had a new sheen on it. One of the painters had been working on repairing the panelling since 5.00 that day, It now looked like a protective wooden castle wall keeping the customers safe. It went all the way around the new restaurant and had taken on a beauty in its own right.

Doug who had been home and came back again was just astonished at the amount of work that had been accomplished in one day. He noticed that kitchen tops had been fitted, and the kitchen equipment was commissioned with both electric and water services. The two carpenters were already fitting the wall cupboards. Large gas hobs and ovens were being fitted as he looked.

The plumber had managed to bring in his pal, a gas-fitter, who was connecting the supplies to the cookers, whilst Helen, the electrician, stood ready to connect the electrics. In the centre of the kitchen, stood an island worktop in black marble laid out and ready to be permanently fitted. The other plumber was busy connecting water supplies to the large Belfast sinks for food preparation.

The service hatches had serving shelves that the customers' food would be placed on when service was ready to go out.

Doug just looked on. He still had to pinch himself. He saw Claire and Fern painting away at the ceiling which had been brought back into life with a new covering of white satin paint. It looked so clean and refreshing. He just smiled at them as there were no words that could cover what he wanted to say.

"Maurice, you and your men must be exhausted!" Doug stuttered. He knew full well that the description of exhausted would not cover the way they felt after a sixteen-hour shift or so.

"No, not really, it's at the end of the job we feel that way to be quite honest. All we feel at the moment is the pride and passion we have for ourselves and the respect of the theatre staff."

Then women started arriving through the exit door. They carried carpet cleaning machines with them. Maurice introduced them. They were the cleaners that worked on the ships before they were launched. The cleaning equipment was from the yard; they had spirited it away to the community centre and club before it could be destroyed by the overseers of the closures, who weren't really interested in the small things around the closing of the docks. They only dealt with big money items.

Five women were now in the building site. "This is Doris, my trouble and strife." Maurice then introduced all the women by using their Christian names. "They've dropped off the carpet machines for tomorrow. The carpets haven't been cleaned for years," he said. "But looking at them, they are still in good condition."

An assessment the women agreed with. "Doug, do you have any more step-ladders?" Doris and the four women wanted to start cleaning the chandeliers as they were filthy. Tomorrow, Helen will check out all the wiring and test them.

Claire phoned down to the basement and the ever-reliable Geoff quickly appeared with step-ladders. "Hi, Claire, as requested. Step-ladders. My goodness, it looks so different in here already."

The women who had appeared suddenly, quickly set to work. They had all the equipment they needed. Also, a special glass cleaning fluid. Immediately, the crystal that made up the chandeliers began to sparkle and returned to their original status. The ingrained smoke and the forty years or so of lack of loving attention was soon being removed as the woman on the ladder moved eloquently around the crystal teardrops with her hands covered by yellow plastic gloves.

Soon, the late Victorian teardrop pieces and black iron arms with touches of gold leaf that held the complex decorations on them were quickly coming back to life again. It was like watching a magic lantern show as the group of women together brought the chandeliers back to life. Chandelier after chandelier was brought lovingly back to its original beauty.

Helen, the electrician, had already audited the lights and noted how many candle-type lightbulbs she would need, but the work could wait until the next day.

At 9.30 or so, Doug and Maurice called a halt. The team said their goodbyes and left the building by the same exit route they had arrived by, with the departing words from Maurice, "Same time tomorrow, folks, and don't be late, so get some sleep. By this time tomorrow night, we can relax a little. Or hopefully we can."

Doug pulled the fire doors shut behind them, ensuring they were closed properly and the alarm was triggered and armed. After which he left the building and walked to his car. He looked up at the autumn skies and saw that the stars appeared brighter tonight for some reason, against the seasonal darkness.

He smiled thoughtfully to himself of how, even as the problems they encountered that long day had intensified, it felt that somehow they were spiritually navigated and resolved. And in essence by allowing people's true characters to shine through. Human characteristics, he thought, that were made of courage and determination to do the right things today. Showing how humanity and a real togetherness can become a force for good. Even more so in times of people's desperation.

In anyone's book, it was one of those rare days that being human meant something good, something tangible, and something meaningful. Mr Collingwood headed home for another meal sitting warm in the oven.

Chapter XIV
Workers to the Rescue

The only way to do great work
is to love what you do.

Steve Jobs

Wednesday morning at 4.00 precisely, the fire doors were flung open for day two of project 'Fix It', as Maurice had nicknamed it. Quickly, the workers assembled around a table. Doug thought they looked remarkably refreshed given the time they finished last night. In the café, the coffee kid had already turned the large urns of water onto the highest setting and was preparing the coffee machine.

He was even more determined to do his bit today. For after leaving work the previous night, and for reasons he was not sure, he went home and sat with his old grandmother and told her what happened that very day to him at work. Together, they talked like they never had before. She remembered clearly the old electric light theatre on Ruby Street and how, when she was younger, most couples did their courting over a good movie.

The bairns of the parish, she recalled, had a Saturday morning matinee for a half penny. "Before the war, there were at least one hundred electric theatres around the toon you know," she told her grandson Richard. "The Deco was just one of them. But a plush place, it was." She spoke warmly to him with a passion in her voice he had never heard before.

"There were at least six in Whitley Bay down at the coast yah know." She continued to reminisce about the past in a happy dream-like way that Richard had never seen before. She searched her memory to find her fading past. She spoke in whispers and told him how the family would travel to the coast every summer for a one-day holiday. "How we looked forward to that day. It was such a special day for all the family."

Granma Martha produced a photo or two from her old handbag that always sat beside her favourite chair. She handed Richard the pictures and pointed out who all his great uncles and aunts were. With tears welling up in her eyes, she recalled with sadness that following the war, half of the people in the photographs had gone. "Disappeared totally! The price of war is a costly one son and even more so for the poor," she said gazing at the picture in her old wrinkled hands.

"After the war, these theatres became even more lovely places. Bright electric lights everywhere. Ornate plaster decorations that look like icing sugar and the tallest of mirrors. Mostly owned by American film studios if I remember rightly." The old lady continued, "A time, son, in history when even the poorest of the parish could feel a little bit special for just a few half-pennies."

Richard listened with great intensity to what his gran had to say. He had never seen her so engaging but these memories of what he had seen that day had sparked something in her. An inner happiness that shone across her face. He held her hand for the first time ever and just listened to her talk about bygone days of her youth and missed opportunities.

He was glad he had spoken to her that night, as opposed to his usual passing niceties of a quick 'Hi Gran!' whilst on his way to his room to get ready to go out.

Early that morning, or perhaps one could say the middle of the night, the group of volunteer workers and theatre staff once again congregated in the restaurant. This time, it included the cleaning ladies with their old dockyard skills ready to be employed. The workers quickly broke out into the various groups and trades so as to carry on the now important refurbishment work, so that it could re-open its doors as planned on Friday evening. Two days away.

"Doug," Maurice said looking at him. "We will probably need another trip to the trade centre today if that's OK. Can I use my Fern and your Claire again?"

"Of course, Maurice," replied Doug. "And again I can't thank you enough. The amount and quality of work you got through yesterday was just staggering. No, more of a miracle really. I wouldn't have known where to start."

They surveyed the room and kitchen together. Now standing side by side, they watched Fern and Claire. Once again rolling the large ceiling with soft satin white paint. Maurice knew that the finish could only get better with more coats of paint the two women added. A finish that was certainly befitting the Art Deco Restaurant.

"You know, Doug, young Fern was up before me this morning. Made tea and toast for both me and the wife. Goodness knows what's got inside her head. But let's hope for more of it."

"I'm glad. What I've seen of her, she's been a great help to Claire and you should be proud of her! How old is she?"

"Eighteen in November and her whole life ahead of her. That is if I could keep her more focused." Maurice removed his cap and wiped his brow out of habit. "Well, Doug. What you just said about her is something I thought I would never hear anyone say about our Fern. She's quite a handful usually. And very set in her ways, and certainly can't abide fools, and knows when she's being treated like one."

"You should see her in action with the suppliers at times who have let us down in the past. She has an answer for everything. And most times, she's right. Unfortunately, mature people take this as her being rude. If anything, she's too quiet at times when she should speak up for herself. Instead, she just walks off in a huff usually."

With that, the two men from entirely different backgrounds separated and went their different ways. Doug walked back to the chambers in quiet anticipation of a possible opening on Friday. He had not cancelled the opening. As he felt deep down inside that this could be pulled off by these unique invisible ex-shipyard workers.

At around 9.00 precisely, the coffee kid brought up food for the workers. He noticed the women were cleaning the eighth and last chandelier and they gleamed and sparkled like they were new. He thought about some of the comments his gran had made the night before and smiled. How these theatre restaurants in the past were usually reserve for the wealthier and more privileged of society.

He looked at the gold letters that made up the sign on the smoking room door, '**Gentlemen Only**' it pronounced. He thought of his gran and the not so well-off punters in the cheap seats, most likely sharing a pavement outside for a smoke in the rain. He placed the large tray of food on the table and with his assistant for the day in tow, another tray was added. His assistant was a very young girl called Suzie.

Who, it has to be said, wanted quite clearly to go home from the moment she arrived. And incidentally was on a hospitality course at a nearby college, but did not know why as she had asked to do a hair and beauty course. Now on the table sat a mound of bacon, egg and sausage sandwiches. The coffee kid was quick to recognise that the food tastes of these workers and their visiting trades people was very different from that of the usual punters.

Today, the sandwiches flew off the trays and using mugs instead of cups. It all seemed more akin to the taste of these wonderful trades people. Fern was holding a large mug of tea in one hand while she cut along the border with a three-inch brush in her other hand. Richard noticed her cutting in line was perfectly straight and did not touch the wood panelling that separated the two areas of the wall. She must have covered about eight feet without lifting the brush.

Claire handled the mug of tea and bacon sandwich with a delicacy more attuned to a breakfast wrap and cappuccino. This was not lost on Fern, and a second later, they were both laughing at each other. Claire covered with paint and Fern not a dash on her.

Claire left the building site, or more correctly the new restaurant. She agreed the previous day to meet Richard Cobbler, the restaurant manager. From talking to him on the phone, she had instinctively felt he was a genuine type of person. She went to the coffee shop that edged the pavement of the outside world run now by the other Richard. Only large panes of glass separated street life and the coffee shop dwellers.

At the same time, Richard Cobbler arrived with a smile. She thought he must be about twenty years her senior. He congratulated her on the promotion. They shook hands and at the same time, Richard said, "You deserved it and don't let anyone tell you any different. You can't keep Chinese whispers in a box in this place."

"Not Fern?" Claire said with a surprise.

He quickly answered, "Fern who?"

They both walked up the stairs. Richard was wearing denim jeans, a casual t-shirt and thin waterproof jacket. "Do you want to see the kitchen and restaurant first?"

He looked at her. "The last time I looked in there, it was a wreck of a place and I can't imagine it being anything else in just two days."

"Well, you're in for a surprise then." She opened the restaurant doors and they stepped inside. She could see he was physically taken aback by what he saw. The transformation was so incredible. Claire made him put on a hard hat, and together she introduced him to Maurice, the magician, and his wizard team.

You could see that Richard was not really listening to anything she said as he was still registering mentally his new empire.

"Richard, you come up when you're ready and we can have a meeting with Mr Collingwood. He's in the trustees' chambers dealing with the invites for Friday."

Richard never spoke and could only nod. He and Maurice, the plumber, Helen, the electrician, and a fitter became a group in the kitchen. Richard was pointing at things whilst at the same time turning on the water taps over the sinks situated in the marbled island preparation area.

Claire was back in the office looking through the draws when she noticed that they were three large cardboard boxes sealed up behind the office door. At that moment, there was a knock on the door and Fern walked in. "I have a list of stuff that Uncle Maurice needs. He says the handles of the cupboards are missing so we need to go to two outlets so we get a better deal."

"Ok, Fern, let's go. By the way, what's in the boxes?"

Fern looked at the boxes, "Oh them. The precious table-cloths and things that belong to the theatre. You know the things you had a bee in your bonnet about. Do you know the people who borrowed them said that they were so busy and could we pick them up? I gave him a little advice about how on loan supply chain system works in reality.

"It must have worked because he brought them in this morning, personally. He promised that they had all been washed and pressed. I told him that you would be over if he lied and you are not to be messed with. He said he can't wait to meet you! I think he was being funny but who cares, we got the missing stuff back.

"As you said, Ms Claire, it's actions this week and not words that count, and where I'm from, that means everything. We're so used to hearing just words, loads of them followed by broken promises. Well, that's what Uncle Maurice and his mates say. I haven't made my mind up yet to be honest."

"Let's go then, Fern, or Uncle Maurice will be on our backs before we know it."

Claire, the acting manager, and Fern, her forthright assistant, returned two hours later with the parts and things on the list. They delivered them to Maurice via the fire exit. Fern got on with whatever Uncle Maurice directed. Claire was going to find Richard. Although, whilst walking across the restaurant floor, she noticed the cleaning ladies had two industrial carpet cleaning machines at work.

Claire was in all honesty lost for words about how the tartan carpet had been restored to its original colours. She also noticed that the used water and cleaner fluid which had gathered in the hopper was absolutely filthy. By now, nothing would surprise her about the dozen or so people here, that had effectively rescued the Art Deco from the edge of becoming a bit of a laughing stock, if truth be known.

She tapped on the chamber door and "Enter" came as the response. Richard Cobble, Mr Douglas Collingwood, and Claire Smith settled down for a catch-up. Mr Cobble was still a little overwhelmed by what he had seen.

Doug broke the silence. "But will it be ready for the opening and can you get your staff back in time?" He asked the pointed question of Richard.
"Apart from the Hobart potato peeler and one steamer we are ready to cook in the kitchen." He continued as he examined a grubby piece of paper in his hands. "The new ovens have been tested and the thermostat readings are perfect and they are ready to cook with. Fridges and cool room temperatures are all in sync too. Where did you get these people from, Mr Collingwood?

"Their workmanship is second to none. Areas which health and safety inspectors always pick up have all been dealt with, drains and scuppers are fitted and fixed superbly."

The sealant around the edges of everything is perfect and will be cured by tomorrow and ready to use. Doug shared that Maurice, the magician, had told him, "They had dealt with every type of problem a galley space will throw at you when working onboard large liners that they built. And everything had to be perfect for the owners." Doug used the words of Maurice. "After a while, it is the only way they know how to do things. To perfection."

Richard then asked, "What happened to all the beautiful pot plants that were in the old cafe and in all areas of the building actually? They were beautiful mature indoor plants and trees."

No one answered for a moment and then Claire spoke, "I think I know where they are. They're at the Evening Gazette's offices."

"You think?"

"I'll check with Evie; she's coming over for a coffee and a catch-up later." The conversation continued. Doug reported, "They now have the original gold-framed photos of the old building and restaurant in the cellar. Apparently, the scenery painters, feeling a little left out, have refurbished the frames with gold leaf and cleaned the glass in them. Hopefully, by the end of play tomorrow, we'll have them back and hung on their original fittings in the restaurant."

Richard leaned forward in the chair. "I still don't believe it. Well, I'm of to the Wheat Market to confirm our order for tomorrow. I promised Maurice I'll be in early tomorrow to go over a snagging list with him. He said it won't be a big list. Well that will make a change," said Richard with a hint of sarcasm in his voice.

The day ploughed on and with every hour, the restaurant started to show the classic art deco features and take on the air of a classy place to eat. The painting was finished and walls and ceilings looked like new. The wood panelling against the duck egg blue walls and startling white ceiling looked the part.

Seemingly, the walls originally had fresco styled paintings along the whole length of them but they were destroyed in the war and no one had a picture of the original. "What a shame," said Claire.

Thursday, and day three of the refurbishment, finally arrived and after the two previous long working days, the place looked like it could open tomorrow, but Maurice pointed out what needed to be finished. Richard, the coffee kid, as the workers had nicknamed him and who was now part of the team, was there as early as everyone. This time with Suzie, his make-shift assistant.

The rolls had been replaced today by thickly cut slices of white bread covered in brown sauce. The workmen warmed to these immediately. Nothing like a bit of bacon and eggs before you get started.

And there it was by 4.00 that Thursday evening, Maurice proudly handed over the reins of the kitchen to Richard Cobble. Who, it had to be said, was still lost for words, but had his own idea of how to say something of worth in return. He and his staff took over the kitchens. Richard had planned for this day over the last nine long months or so. And in all honesty, at times he felt he should move on as nothing seemed to be happening, but now he was glad he hadn't.

He and his staff were donned in chef's whites and checks. And in their appropriate footwear, they moved about the kitchen whilst they familiarised themselves where everything was. They looked to find where the main electrical switch boxes were and started recording the fridge temperatures. They were like children in a sweetie shop.

"Richard, come here," suddenly a woman in chef's whites shouted. "Look at this. It's a miracle." The chef showed Richard, the dumb waiter. "Look it works, it really works. We can send stuff down to the coffee shop without constantly running up and down those ruddy flights of stairs." The kitchen staff stood around in a semi-circle looking at the dumb waiter that had not worked for as long as anyone could remember.

By now, Helen, and the best electrician in the world, smiled. "I thought you would like that one."

In the dining area, and with Richard overseeing the ladies, the large round dark mahogany tables and chairs were slowly set out for service in an order that followed the layout presented on one of the old photographs. Now back and hanging in their original places. The dining chairs that had been in the smoking room were being passed along by a chain of people all wishing to help.

At the same time, about ten people arrived from the paper with Evelyn in charge, and through the fire escape delivered a range of indoor plants and trees. "For the new Art Deco Restaurant as ordered by Ms Claire Smith," Evie shouted out. At the same time, the workers all applauded as one. They had looked a proper spectacle walking down the city centre lined with shops and shoppers, but they had brought a few smiles to their many faces as these walking forests moved along.

Even adding a grin to the face of a hardened traffic warden. Richard guided them to where they used to stand. On the walls, the old pictures of the 1940's cafe had been re-hung. Richard manoeuvred the new plants to the very same position to where they originally stood if possible. In the good old days as some would say.

Evelyn and Claire had paired off and sauntered back to her office on the top floor. As she looked at her bottle of water on the desk, Claire reflected, "Well, it's Thursday again and it's been one hell of a mad week for both of us, Evie girl. Trips to Ireland, missing people, strange people, good people, grumpy people, young people and old people, we've met them all, Evie."

The two women sat on chairs facing each other across the desk. "How you getting on with Mr Cousins?" Claire asked.

"Well, he still calls me Ms Borowski in the morning, but I do catch a glimpse of Evelyn, usually when I'm fetching him something. But I do realise he knows everything about journalism and he and Mort felt they took a great risk sending us to the hinterland of Ireland."

"Really! I thought it was lovely and I must look up that artist's name when I get a chance," Claire responded.

"What artist?" Evie replied.

"The artist that painted those excellent watercolours that lined the corridor outside of our bedrooms at the Manor Guesthouse." Claire used the tone of a schoolmistress. "The name given was an R Esaw."

Evie broke in, "What time you finishing today?"

"I don't know" replied Claire. " Probably about 'late' again I would think, and you. We have the VIPs dinner and the official opening of the new Old Art Deco Theatre restaurant tomorrow. It says 19.00-22.00 on the invitation. I'm not sure what my part will be. I'm sure Rachael Cummins would have played a major role but Mr Collingwood hasn't said anything."

Evie chipped in. "The same for me. I'm going back to the office and check through my article one more time before I print it off and let Frank see it tomorrow morning. He doesn't even have an email address you know!"

"What about Louisa?"

"No word. Mr Mortimer has had no luck finding her in London. None of his contacts have seen hide nor hare of her. And apparently, she never turned up for her interview last week either. I think everyone is now more than a little concerned for the woman."

Evie was seen out of the building by Claire and the two chatted for a while on the pavement outside. The bright lights of the bars and restaurants, busy traffic and bustle of pedestrians made it look exciting and inviting. They both noticed that the nights were beginning to draw in quickly.

Claire visited the basement and workshops. Ever-reliable Geoff was in the basement. Claire thought he must live there. He was rewinding large spools of film from one to another for showing on the older projectors.

Geoff welcomed the company and they spoke about everything that had happened to get the restaurant back in action. Ever reliable Geoff was pleased as it would draw more people in, and they often stayed on for a movie or a bit of theatre. More seats were sold when the cafe was open upstairs; now a very stylish café, he added.

She moved to the scenery workshops where four volunteers were painting away on large canvasses, creating a winter wonderland for the pantomime they were showing this year.

In the foyer, the public milled around, some just fascinated by the Art Deco features, others purchasing tickets for the cinema.

She returned to the fourth floor at around 7.30 and Mr Collingwood was in the oak panelled passageway.

"Here you are. I was just looking for you. Come in."

She sat down in the chambers and Richard, the restaurant manager, was already in attendance and sat on one of the fine chairs. Doug opened the conversation. "Well, this time tomorrow, the guests for the opening night of the new restaurant will be arriving. Claire, I hope you will do the meet and greet as the manager. Richard, how's the preparations coming for the night?"

"All in hand, starters and desserts are basically done and mains will be completed tomorrow afternoon. We'll be ready to plate up and serve at 8.00 pm. Pre-drinks will be served beforehand in the small cinema area. Guests will be invited to sit down at 07.50 where the starters will be already in place." Richard's maturity and clear voice presented a confidence that all would be ready for the opening night.

Doug went through the invitations' list. "Two of our benefactors have dropped out as they had to go to the Bahamas on a business trip but did send a donation for the theatre." He handed a cheque for ten thousand pounds to Claire. "Can you bank that and take care to record it and draft out a nice thank you letter? I'll sign it next week sometime."

Doug continued, "I see that the journalist from the Evening Gazette is not invited. What's her name?"

Claire replied, "Evelyn Borowski."

"And Mr Mortimer is still in London?"

"Yes. He's still looking for his daughter and he is really worried. It's nearly two weeks since she was last heard from."

"That's worrying for a father," Doug came back.

He leant over the desk and picked up the phone, got an outside line and rang a number.

"Hi, Frank, how are you? No news about Louisa yet."

"None. I spoke to Mort today," replied Frank. "He's still in London looking up old contacts and working with the police now. It'll be two weeks on Monday. We are all really worried over here now. Anyway, how can I help you?"

Doug and Frank spoke for a while and then Doug told Frank what he had phoned up for. "Can you come instead of Mort and what's her name, instead of Louisa. The Evening Gazette has been good to us and we would like your company." There was more banter between them, which to sum it up was Frank asking Doug if it was going to be one of those terrible non-alcoholic affairs. "No, Frank, there'll be drinks and a free dinner."

"It's not black tie, is it?" Frank asked cynically.

"No, but my wife's brushing off my lounge suit so I won't get away with it. So, see you between 7 and 7.30 tomorrow."

"Ok, Doug. And I'll pass the good news on to Ms Borowski too." And he put down the phone.

Evelyn, having just got back from the theatre, was just about to sit down when she heard her name being used over the phone. Frank, who on one of those rare occasions was working late, brought her up to date on the current situation and gave her the good news that she would be working tomorrow night; if you can call it working.

Frank advised her to get a few quotes from the rich and famous and publish them in an article about the opening of the Old Art Deco Restaurant. "They love having their names printed in the local rag and keep smiling even at their ridiculous jokes and stories," he said mockingly.

Doug Collingwood put down the phone and said to Claire, "Add Mr Cousins and Ms Borowski to the guest list. We need the press there. Claire, can you knock up a short press release and post it out to our usual press contacts? The list is on the wall of your office somewhere. One other thing, Richard has had an idea he wants to share."

Richard looked at his notepad. "Claire, you know that without Maurice and the old shipyard workers, none of this would have been possible."

Claire nodded in total agreement.

He continued, "The restaurant doesn't actually open up to the public until Tuesday next week. Well, I thought, and my staff agreed to work for free, to put on a good old-fashioned Sunday lunch for all those who helped and their families. What do you think?"

Claire's response was immediate. "Count me in!"

"How many do you think will come?"

"Well, there were five of Maurice's crew, Helen, the electrician, and about four or five women cleaners plus families."

Doug chipped in. "Look, I offered Maurice and his workers some cash but they would not accept it. They were adamant. They were quite clear that being appreciated for their work and how it gave them some dignity and respect back was more than a payment."

Doug continued, "But what I have agreed with Maurice is that the families from the community centre can have free tickets for the pantomime. Maurice stated that they would love that and I want you to book a bus to ferry them back and forth, Claire. It's the least we can do! The money they've saved the theatre is no one's business but it's a lot of money, I'm not sure of the figures yet."

"We'll all have to work Saturday to pull it off but we can't allow what they achieved here to go unrewarded. And between you and me, Claire, can you get your reporter buddy to attend? I know she got photos of the old and new and some of the workers involved. But it won't do us any harm and it would be a bit of fun."

There was a complete agreement between all parties. "One other thing, next week, Claire, we'll have to look at staffing and see how we can utilise all staff and volunteers more, shall we say, be more proactive. They all have good ideas. Let's listen to them."

Richard was now the manager of a fully functional, well-equipped restaurant; Claire, now the acting manager of operations, and Mr Mortimer, chairperson of the board of trustees. All stood up and, before they left the chamber, shook hands and congratulated themselves, and all looked forward to working with each other and to achieve the success the Old Art Deco Theatre thoroughly deserved.

Chapter XV
Two Dinners Are Better Than One!

Sadly, ideologies separate us.
Dreams and anguish bring us back together…

Eugene Lonesco

At around 7.00 Friday evening, Ms Claire Smith was at her post as agreed previously by Mr Collingwood, and standing in the foyer of the Art Deco Theatre and Cinema, meeting and greeting guests and directing them to the small cinema lounge on the second floor where pre-dinner drinks were being served.

"Hello, Ms Claire Smith. And a very good evening to you." It came from a voice in the crowd. Then suddenly, both Edith and Enid dressed in their fineries were stood there in the foyer of the Art Deco. Claire did not recognise them from the list as they were down as 'Taylors x 2'.

"Hello, Edith and Enid, and welcome to the opening night dinner." They both returned a sweet smile and at the same time, passed her two presents both wrapped in brown paper and bound in string. One addressed 'To Ms Borowski' and the other 'To Ms Smith'. *How formal,* Claire thought.

"Has Louisa Mortimer appeared yet?" Ms Enid Taylor, the smaller said.

"No, not yet, everyone is really, really worried now," Claire whispered.

The two ladies, still dressed liked characters from a 1940s play, were escorted to the lift by Claire. It has to be noted though very stylish in the midst of a modern society. Their hair was immaculate and they wore strings of pearls around their necks, and had large green broaches that twinkle brightly in the soft Italian lighting. They immediately cast a glance at each other and one could not miss it was a grimacing concerning glance.

Claire directed them into the lift and gave them the directions to the lounge where drinks were being served. Edith, the taller, laid a hand on hers and thanked her again, but in a way that said that they were now all connected somehow. Claire, on her part, thanked them again for their presents and told them that Evelyn was attending tonight as well. "Oh, that's good. Very good!"

The guests kept arriving in twos, threes and fours and eventually Claire recognised a voice she knew. "Hello, Ms Borowski. How good that you could make it. We are honoured." Claire spoke with oodles of sarcasm.

Frank, standing close behind Evie, interrupted, "Press." Giving Evelyn a side look.

Claire, quick as a flash, responded, "Of course, you are, Mr Cousins. And the theatre welcomes you and your profession to the opening night dinner at the Art Deco Restaurant. It's a great pleasure to have you here," Claire said with a mischievous look in her eye.

Frank burst out laughing at this. "Just show me where the drinks are and leave the patter to your mate here. She'll be writing the piece, not me!"

Claire turned towards Evie. "You'll never guess who's here?" Without waiting for an answer from Evie, said, "Edith and Enid from the Manor. I never knew that they were supporters of the old theatre at any level. They brought us both a present too!"

By now, you could see Frank was bored of the small chatter and pulling Evie away and in the direction of where the drinks were located. Shortly afterwards, Frank and Doug were talking like they were long-lost buddies. Evelyn spotted the Taylor twins and made a bee-line for them and said hello. They talked and caught up on things that had taken place over the week.

The twins both thought that the help from the retired trades people was such a marvellous endeavour. They both hoped that the theatre would reward them in a suitable fashion. Evelyn shared with them the plan they had for Sunday. Also, the donated pantomime tickets for the families from the community centre on the scheme where the trades and crafts people still lived and married.

They were thrilled by the approach of the theatre staff. Especially the notion that they were giving up their own free time to make it work. The conversation changed slightly to Louise Mortimer and her disappearance, which as Claire had already picked up on, physically worried the Taylor women. "Is her father still in London?"

"Yes," Evie replied. Again, wondering how they knew so much.

"Well, let's hope she turns up safe and sound soon. We can understand how worried her father must be," Enid replied with a warm caring smile on her face.

Another elderly couple came over and it was obvious that they wanted to speak to the two ladies.

"I must circulate and get a few comments to quote. I'm press now you know." She smiled at Edith and Enid and the two women acknowledged her happiness. They both wished her well with her work. Quickly adding, "No journalism," and said they would speak to her later.

As she moved away, Frank grabbed Evie's arm. "Who are those two old birds?"

"There from the Manor Guesthouse in Ireland. They were working with Louisa on something. Something to do with the documentary film we believe. You know the one Mr Mortimer passed to Clive, the gardener, at The Gazette on Monday."

"Really," said Frank with a quizzical look on his face. At that, he moved on to some other poor unsuspecting sole that had caught his eye. Evelyn did wonder how he knew so many people, but he and Mr Collingwood and Mr Mortimer did go back a long way in the city, or so it appeared.

The dinner could only be described as divine. Richard and his staff had been on top form and they had kept their word. Everything went so smoothly. Claire sat at a table with guests and sponsors and noticed that Fern was now waiting on the tables too. She looked in fascination as her new assistant lifted the finished plates onto her forearm like a professional waitress.

She must have had eight plates at a time balancing up her forearm. *Is there no end to the skills of that girl?* She thought. They gave each other a nod and knowing glance. Fern moved closer to her ear, "Is madam finished with her dessert?"

Turning her head towards Fern, she replied, "Yes, madam has." Claire gave her a cheeky wink and a nod. Fern grinned back at her and although, loaded up with dirty plates, moved away in an effortless style. After which she disappeared into the kitchen through the swing doors by walking backwards.

The after-dinner speeches came fast and furious and everyone applauded each other as they do on these occasions. Although, it has to be said that, there was a real positive vibe around the room. They all felt the future of the Art Deco with its new refurbished restaurant would give the city a refreshing buzz, and the standard of the food would attract the foodie types through their doors. Or so the local paper would report.

At that point, they all raised their glasses and toasted the kitchen and table staff. Richard, the manager, responded with a few words. Claire was surprised by how elegantly he spoke to the audience. He mentioned to the audience that so many of his staff, whom were still in their early teens, had done an outstanding job that evening.

Richard ended with, "And if they stay focused, would surely have excellent careers in the future. If they keep applying themselves through hard work." The audience of dignitaries agreed wholeheartedly and tapped the table lightly shouting at the same time 'Here! Here!'. Evie looked over at Frank who was necking someone else's wine and anything else he could get his hands on by the look of it.

Before anyone had time to take it all in, the evening had come to an end all too quickly. It had already gone on for about forty-five minutes longer than planned.

The staff started to bring in the coats of many designs and descriptions. People were already putting them on and saying their last farewells to each other under the now gleaming and glowing chandeliers.

Edith and Enid came over and spoke to both Evelyn and Claire, sharing with them that their evening had been, "Just wonderful. The vibrancy of the place, so full of young people with so much energy and so many positive thoughts for the future, all being shared between young and old alike. It's so wonderful to see. Well, we are travelling back first thing in the morning. We've got guests arriving tomorrow from Israel.

"Well, we must meet up again. And soon! If you and Claire want to come and stay again at the Manor over the winter months, then you would be most welcome. Just let us know and we'll make all the travel arrangements. Keep us posted, Evie, about Ms Mortimer. Like many others, we are really worried about her.

"And thanks for returning the film last week, Claire, it was so important to us. There were parts of it that are irreplaceable evidence." The women smiled back at the two ladies.

The four said their goodbyes and moved off in their own directions in perhaps the hope of regaining their own individuality to some degree.

The following day being Saturday, Evelyn woke at around 7.00, walked around the park, and then grabbed some breakfast. About 8.30, Stig woke up and come out of his room. "Well hello, stranger. They are certainly getting their money's worth out of you at that paper."

"It's been a bit of a funny old week. In fact, I'm going in today to help Claire get ready for another do at the theatre tomorrow."

"Best mates now, hey!"

"You're right, we do get on well. I've really only had one friend before. Her name was Rosie. We were in care together, but she let me down big time. I let her sofa surf one night as she was really stuck for somewhere to sleep. She got up after the other students left for lectures and lifted a load of things from them. As you can imagine, it didn't go down well.

"I nearly lost my place at university through her, and nobody really forgave me for allowing her to stay. Hence life lesson number one, trust no one I suppose."

Stig replied, "Well, we all do stupid mad things once in a while. And you don't strike me as the unforgiving type deep down inside either."

At that point, they could hear a car horn tooting in the background. Evie looked out of the window and Claire was outside, a little earlier than agreed.

"Evie, are you in tonight? I'm having a couple of friends over to watch the match," Stig asked.

"No problem," Evie said, "and I should be back early evening I would think. But no problem. I can already hear my bed calling."

For the rest of the day, the two women, Richard, the restaurant manager, and his staff, straight-talking Fern, and Richard, the coffee kid, helped set up for tomorrow's special Sunday lunch for the brilliant workers and their families. Doug had discussed the details and reasoning with Maurice who eventually agreed; but not without some persuading it has to be said.

He said that with his wife, Doris, and some husbands, it meant that about thirty were coming. Doug asked if any of them were vegetarian. Maurice replied, "Of course, they all eat vegetables with their meat and potatoes." One of Richard's chefs was busy making various types of trifles which she would finish with whipped cream before serving tomorrow.

The theatre's second round of guests would start arriving at around 12.00 and would be sitting down by 1.00. In the small lounge, the white and red wines from the evening before had been supplemented by cans of lagers and beer being added to the cold shelves.

Eight tables were prepared. Pristine white tablecloths covered the mahogany wood and six fine chairs were placed around each one.

Claire, Fern and Evelyn worked together in harmony. "Fern."

"Yes, Ms Claire," Fern replied. Claire shot her a look.

Fern walked over to her. "Fern, what do you think if we put some flowers on the tables in the middle? Do you think they would look nice? Not too over the top?"

"Ok. How many bunches do you want? My aunt works in the indoor market across the way behind the shopping mall. She'll let us have them for cost. Or at least a bit cheaper as it's Saturday, and I won't let her rip you off."

Claire looked at Fern. *What is it with this girl, she seems to have a relative for every occasion and her thing about being ripped off!*

"In the cash box upstairs. The one in the top draw of my desk. Take fifty pounds and see what you can get us," Claire casually said.

Fern looked puzzled. "You want me to take the money out the cash box myself. How much is in it?" She enquired.

"About two hundred pounds," Claire replied. "Why?" Fern went quiet.

"Look, Fern, if we are to work closely together, we need total trust and loyalty in everything we do together. I don't let you down and you don't let me down. OK."

Fern nodded her head in silent agreement then added, "Can I take the coffee kid with me? And by the way, he would like to bring his gran tomorrow as she met his grandad at the pictures here. He's now dead and she has great memories of this place." Fern was as direct as ever.

Richard looked embarrassed. "I told you not to say anything."

"Well," Fern retorted, "Ms Claire isn't anyone. She is a manager and my uncle says I have to listen and learn everything from her. As she is a good manager and you don't get many of them nowadays." This remark was followed by one of those strangely quiet moments.

Evelyn was chuckling away to herself. Claire shot her a look as to say shut up. The coffee kid was still red-faced and Fern just carried on folding napkins like nothing had happened.

"Get some flowers for the table. Please take the money out of the cash box but get a receipt for everything you spend."

"Will do. Shall I get mixed colours or stay with red? They would look lovely against the pristine white tablecloths."

"Red would be just great. But just nice flowers and if there are not enough red ones that would be great too."

"Okay. Consider it done. Actions not words, Ms Claire."

After Richard and Fern left, Evelyn spoke, "Where did you get her from. Is there anything she can't get hold of?"

"She's been both a trooper this week and a thorn in my side at the same time. Give her a job and it certainly gets done. I think Richard and some of the staff are slightly nervous of her…and at the same time strangely envious of her. Obviously, Fern can't see that. Doug promised Maurice that we would find her a job here. I'm going to take her on as my assistant.

"She does have a funny way about her though. But she is as quick as a flash and as sharp as a knife. Even if you don't see it at first."

"Perhaps maybe a little too sharp," Evie warned with a raised eye.

"Anyway, apparently Edith and Enid both said to look after her. She'll be an asset in the future. Goodness knows how the Taylor twins seemed to know everything about everyone. Did you open your present, the book? Did you see what it had written in ink inside the cover?"

"Yes." Evie repeated the words verbatim from memory:

To the two wonderful young women who visited The Entity at the Manor Guesthouse. Both wolves in sheep's clothing. All the best for the future from Edith and Enid Taylor (and the colonel and gardeners). P.S. Chapter 16 will be of interest.

The book, given as a present to each, was titled *Nietzsche and the Nazis* by a writer called Stephen Hicks. "Obviously, they want us to read it, especially something to do with chapter 16," said Evie.

The two women were more than slightly puzzled by everything that had happened to them in the last couple of weeks. The book, the sponsorship for Claire by the society, the knowledge that Doug had shared with them. For it was this society whom the Taylor twins were a major part of, and are now the new wealthy patrons of the Art Deco; and they are also financially supporting her paid post for three years.

"I wonder what it's all about," Claire replied. "Not that I'm moaning."

"It's obvious that the Taylor twins and the colonel are part of some society or foundation that operates from the Manor Guesthouse," said Evie. She continued, "Whatever it does, it will be harmless I suspect."

Claire agreed. "I think you're right and I'll read the book as soon as I have time and then we can discuss it perhaps. If there is something pointed in the chapter that they highlighted, we must find out what it is. I wonder if it's connected to the documentary they made."

"All seems a bit deep. You're not a conspiracy theorist, are you, Claire?" Both women just laughed and carried on finishing off laying out the dinner tables for the following day.

Suddenly, Claire piped up, "Can you remember the way they told me on the Sunday morning to stay with the theatre as things were going to change quickly for me? And it has, and how did they know that?"

By the end of the afternoon, everything that needed to be done for tomorrow and for the second grand opening of the Old Art Deco Theatre restaurant, was done. The food prepared, the tables set, and there was just as much excitement in the staff's voices. The chefs had busied themselves cooking off lamb, beef and chicken. There was an option available if they did not eat meat. But the chefs felt it was very unlikely.

Every table had a lovely bouquet of red flowers that sat in a low glass vase of water and they looked even more vibrant set against the white table clothes. The silver spoons and black placemats looked so royal. Each one regimentally in place as Fern had instructed Richard, the coffee kid, to do.

Claire phoned Doug and said, "Everything is set for the second launch tomorrow, and everyone had done the Art Deco Theatre proud again. The staff pulled together and a stream of them had come in on their day off to show their support."

Richard locked up the restaurant and they all retired to the coffee shop, where everyone was bought a drink. Fern asked for a bottle of lager which was changed to a soft drink on the instructions of Claire. "Not until you're eighteen, Fernie girl. In November, I believe? On that day, you will get a drink with the compliments of the management team, but not until then."

As always, Fern took everything in her stride and said, "That's fine by me. And I won't forget. Does that mean I will still be here?"

After about half an hour, the team broke up and agreed that the kitchen and restaurant staff would come in at 09.30. The rest would be in for 11.00 to welcome their regal guests. Fern shared with the group around the table, "The people up the scheme are buzzing about the families coming here tomorrow and the tickets for the panto and everything. Uncle Maurice was even looking for his best pair of shoes."

They all felt proud at being invited to eat in a room they only dreamed about when they were younger. Maurice said that to her "…that all things come to those who wait lass." Aunt Doris agreed totally.

Fern, and in her own unadulterated fashion, added, "It's good that it has come to them now as they would be dead before long at this rate." No one added anything to her comment and viewed it as the point to move on for the night.

Sunday morning arrived and Evie and Stig met over the breakfast bar. Stig still amazed at the work rate of Evie and her pal, Claire.

"I'll be back early this evening, Stig. Buy you a drink in the park bar if you would like?" Evie said.

"I thought you would never ask," he said sipping a cup of tea and crunching down on his toast. At that point, the customary car horn hooted. "That'll be Claire." Stig looked up and smiled.

Evie got off the bar stool picked up her bag and headed out for the day.

"Have a good day and look after all those working-class folk. Salt of the earth you know."

"I know and I will," said Evie smiling.

As planned in detail the night before, everything was ready to go by 12 noon exactly. Funnily enough, this time Doug was in the foyer ready to meet and greet the VIPs for the day, plus of course Richard the coffee shop pushing his lovely grandmother in her wheel chair. It was nice to see them all arrive together thought Doug. Men, women, children of the workers, cleaners and Helen, the electrician, and her partner, Ross.

Doug was a great meeter and greeter. "Welcome, everyone. It's a pleasure and an honour to have you all here with us today. For without you people, there would be no today." The guests were quickly shown to the lounge where beer and lager for the men went down well and a little wine for the wives and girlfriends.

Helen, the electrician, and her partner, Ross, must have had at least four cans of lager each in about thirty minutes, and it was evident they could hold their liquor. At the same time, Evie noticed that Frank had slipped into the gathering like a ghost, unnoticed by most but not by Doug, who smiled. "Always a pleasure to have the press attend, Frank."

With him was Tommy, the photographer, with his camera at the ready, and he took some brilliant pictures of the day. The guests could not be happier with a good Sunday roast and a trifle to follow. They had all brushed up really well. They showed their families the work they had completed and around the sleek art deco building.

Helen was still very proud of the fact that she had got the dumb waiter to work. She explained how she had to rewire the motor by hand and replace the brushes and then put it all together again. Helen spoke as a person who was proud of her trade.

"Well done, lass," shouted Maurice. "You done us proud." As nostalgia broke out, all present agreed that there would not be many people who could have done what she did. Helen blushed at the praise being heaped on her.

Unbeknown to the guests, the theatre staff in the basement had put together a treat for them all and they were all guided to the main theatre seats. The coffee kid's grandma, who was wheelchair-bound, was treated like royalty. Two of the young waitressing girls looked after her and pushed her around the theatre. She could remember the main auditorium and it hadn't changed a bit, she told the people gathered.

When all guests were seated and the lights dimmed, the staff raised the curtain and Geoff, the projectionist, showed a fifteen-minute feature that was about the war effort in the Tyne dockyards during the Second World War. This enthralled the families and you could hear them talk about this and that and what had changed.

Their memories of the days after the war when they started their apprenticeships, and also the hardships they had endured over their working lives, were shared with all and sunder.

When the lights came back on again, and to the surprise of the audience, a woman dressed in robes and wearing a chain introduced herself as the City Mayor. She had heard somehow about the work and achievements of the small group of ex-shipbuilders, and she was here as she wanted to express her thanks personally on behalf of the toon. She called Maurice up to the stage and presented him with a plaque with the city's coat of arms.

Maurice was a little taken aback by all this attention, but promised that the plaque would be hung in the community centre as a testimony of the shipbuilding community past and present.

After which they all went back to the dining area for coffee and a brandy if they so wished. *Well, Frank certainly wished*, thought Evie. In fact, he leant over her shoulder and said, "You don't drink," at the same time picking up her glass of brandy. Evie just smiled at roguish Frank and shook her head.

By 4.00, the party began to break up and people started to go their own ways. Doug Collingwood shook hands with Maurice one more time and said, "You sure you won't take anything for your time."

"No, we all agreed. Just having one last chance to show off our skills and do what we've done all our lives is enough. And knowing that our families and the community are so proud of us is more than enough for us all, Doug, before we go to the other side."

After many handshakes and lots of goodbyes, the people who just a week ago were a bunch of total strangers to this world, were now leaving as friends of the theatre. A good day was had by all and the workers would retire back to their working men's club and share stories of what they had seen and what they had achieved in such a short period of time. Maurice would be the butt end of many a joke after being on stage with the mayor.

Two hours later, in the Bar and Coffee house in the city park, Stig, Claire and Evie sat and reflected on the last couple of weeks. Stig remarked, "Do you know, Claire, I've seen your mate at the most three times since our first meeting over a week ago."

She replied, "I've seen more of Evie than I have of my own family this week. Strange how things turn out."

The three sat and chilled for the first time since their coming together. They chatted away about everything and nothing for an hour or so. Stig was the only one drinking alcohol, so he drank for all three of them. The two women just sat and drank soft drinks.

All three wondered where Louisa Mortimer had disappeared to. But that's another story for another edition of the news.

Chapter XVI
The Sad Truth

*Who should be surprised, if the people are not
what they should be or might be?*

Mein Kampf

Around nine weeks had passed since Evelyn first arrived in the North-East to take up her internship at the Newcastle Evening Gazette. Her friendship with Claire and Stig continued to flourish, which was something of a surprise for Miss Evelyn Borowski given her lack of trust of people inherited from her time in care. Now a lot of their spare time was spent visiting local theatres, different cinemas, and other venues around the city.

Meaning she could pen many first-hand accounts on local interest stories about what's on. Evie and Claire always got in for free, and that was nice on its own, as they felt some recognition from others beginning to build in their chosen professions. Having said this, they always left a good tip for the overworked theatre staff.

Evelyn was, as ever, always the journalist, searching for a new and creative storyline. And Claire, the operations manager, always on the hunt for a new idea to sharpen up the theatre's personal standing in the community.

As for Evelyn's internship, she was continually being mentored by Mr Frank Cousins. Who, on some days, was like a colourful butterfly, gentle and fluttery with his ideas and advice. Then on other days, he was like a wasp, ready to sting and rasp at everyone in sight. Louisa Mortimer was still missing and that was beginning to bother her for some reason. Mort, her anxious father, was spending much of his time in London helping the police with their investigation.

Frank continued to support Mort by spending a lot of time on the eighth floor and helping to run the paper and ensuring it met its deadlines. She noticed that the journalist from the eighth floor had started to visit the seventh for a coffee or their lunch break. Most of the exotic indoor plants were now back in situ over at the Art Deco Restaurant, which meant there was more room to rearrange the furniture.

Evelyn and a few of the other journalists had decided to clean up the public area outside the offices. The sofa seats were now situated into small groups so people could actually sit and talk. In the centre were various shaped coffee tables from the sixties. The coffee machine, and it has to be pointed out, after many long-drawn-out conversations with the cave women from the sixth floor, had now been upgraded.

The remaining indoor plants had all been re-potted into good size pots using fresh compost. All the staff from the paper, irrelevant of the floor they worked on, helped out by bringing in large second-hand plant pots of various shapes, colours and sizes.

In Evie's own time and with her soft handling and sensitive care, the beautiful and mature lush green plants slowly became alive again and a new vigorous growth was appearing, making this quiet public space a more inviting one; giving it an appearance of being lived in and looked after. As opposed to a floor full of dust and junk.

Even Mr Frank Cousins commented that it looked much better on the seventh at a daily briefing, and thanked the paper's only intern in five years for her hard work. Evie wasn't sure if he was mocking her or not! But she accepted his compliment on face value.

Returning to the Art Deco, Ms Claire Smith now had her hands firmly on the reigns of the role as operations manager. With the support of Doug Collingwood, the theatre was becoming alive once more, and was no longer just a museum to the past and a place for the wonderful people to be seen. The coffee shop and the Art Deco Restaurant were both doing really well and always full of customers, and it was noted by Fern, always with their array of plastic credit cards at the ready.

Richard, the manager of the restaurant, and his staff had delivered everything they had promised and more. Richard, the coffee shop kid, was making a reputation for himself, always trying new brands and styles of free trade coffee; and with the help of restaurant staff via the much loved and respective dumb waiter, lunch times were becoming busier and busier.

Mr Doug Collingwood was as good as his word and spent three days a week with Claire, and of course, with her ever-reliable sidekick, the dearest Fernie girl.

Evelyn had walked over for lunch and a coffee with Claire, and was just about to enter her office on the top floor, when she was stopped by Mr Collingwood.

"Hello, Ms Borowski. And how are you settling in over at The Gazette? It's been a couple of months roughly, hasn't it? By the way, how's Mort? Any more news about Louisa?"

"No nothing," said Evelyn in a hushed but concerning voice. "…but he's so worried, you can tell. He is in London again helping the police from the missing persons unit. All his old buddies from the papers have circulated her picture and covered the story of a missing journalist whose disappearance has shocked the newspaper world."

"Oh well! Let me know if I can do anything…" Doug's voice kind of trailed off. Probably wondering what he could actually do in reality anyhow. Missing for nine weeks or so, he contemplated to himself, was not good. Facing the reality of the dreadful situation meant some horrible thoughts began to cross his mind for the first time. Thoughts that were really hitting home.

Evelyn stood quietly, and was in fact having the same dire feelings herself but she never shared them with anyone, including Frank or her friends.

Claire and Evie had lunch together in the coffee shop. They spoke about their future plans. In the conversation Claire shared with her that Fern had a right grump on this morning. Apparently, Claire mentioned to her that the board were so impressed by her work, they felt she now deserved some form of job training. Perhaps at a local college or something, but she just shouted, "No. No. Never. Never. Never again!"

And that ended the conversation dead. "She seemed so very angry at the offer of further training, so I just left it at that."

At that moment, Fern walked into the coffee shop. "You just had Thomas Swales on the phone. The guy from the city art gallery. He wanted to talk to you urgently," Fern said in an unusually brash voice, and at the same time, handing Claire the piece of paper with his telephone number on it. Her manner was still harsh and stroppy.

Evie butted in. "Fern, please sit down. We need to talk to you. You know Claire only had your best interest at heart when she suggested further courses and training. Claire admires your work ethos, as we all do. That get-up and go approach you have has touched everyone you come in contact with and everyone just loves you to bits in the theatre. Your energy is contagious and you make them smile. So, what's eating you after Claire mentioned courses?"

All the time Evie's voice was calm and collected. Every word spoken was with a depth of sensitivity that could be well attributed to a person a lot older than Evelyn's twenty-three years.

Still standing, and for a while, Fern stared at the two women. She then slid onto the empty bench space on the other side of the table to them. Claire waved to Richard to bring Fern a cup of coffee. Richard acknowledged the request with a thumbs-up sign.

Fern leant forward and quietly spoke. "Can I ask you where you were both educated and why? And when did you both become such boujee girls?"

Claire and Evie looked at her and sought out the meaning behind the questions. Evie, who was now getting a little agitated, if not thoroughly snappy, looked directly at Fern but with her face retaining the gambler's mask.

She continued, "First of all, Fern, neither Claire or myself are boujee girls. We've worked hard to get where we are. We're definitely not rich and famous because we appeared on some stupid reality TV show or married some overpaid sportsperson. Yes, we both have good degrees and in subjects that have supported our career aspirations. And both incidentally, like you, we had to pass through the mayhem of the Further Education system before reaching Higher Education.

"And Claire didn't mean to insult you. She would never do that, it's not in her nature. But she sees something in you. We all do! You could have a brilliant future. But unfortunately, and there's always a but! If you are not rich, then you are trapped into using the failing education system; which incidentally we both had to work our way through to get where we are today."

Evie looked straight into Fern's face. "At university and because of certain policies, and only because of those policies, people didn't say too much to me about my poor background. But they thought it! And yes, especially the boujee types that hung around the courses I was doing. So, I personally take issue at being called a boujee girl. We are not.

"After leaving the broken care system, we both worked our socks off to get where we are today. We've had no free rides. And neither will you! But you have strength and determination to succeed. To see past the crass class war and woke thing, and look towards your future. And don't get sucked into the self-pitying thing!"

Claire cut in, "What is a boujee girl anyhow?"

Evie snapped, "It's not a compliment. She's dissing us. Check it out on the internet if you like. Anyhow I am not one, Fern! Nor is Claire. If she was, I can tell you straight that I wouldn't be sitting next to her."

Claire, who listened closely to all that was being said, was not sure if this was a compliment or not. Fern sat with an unusual stillness about her; and at the same time, her eyes were welling up with a salty moisture. At that moment, and after all what Evie had just said to her, Fern felt she had let herself down by acting the way she did.

Moreover, for calling out Claire for something she was most definitely not. Claire passed Fern a paper tissue from her pocket and the young woman wiped her eyes, brushing away both the tears and fears for her future with one foul swoop. She giggled to hide her embarrassment. "Christ, I never get emotional yaw know!"

The three laughed at this and then Fern added, "Uncle Maurice always jokes that he was educated once, and it took him a lifetime to get over it. It's a quote he likes to use as a joke by some guy called Mark Twain. I know that Claire means me no harm and wants the best for me, but suggesting that I go back to a local college felt like a real slap in the face for me. And my family.

"They were all so proud of my job here, and going to college is just an insult and a backward step for me and them. The whole estate knows that they are just holding pens for the young chavs and unemployable!"

"What do you want then, Fern?" Evie asked in a quiet and clear voice. A voice showing no intention or emotion. Evie repeated the question again, "What do you want then, Fern?"

"To be like you two, I guess. And that I am listened too for once." Fern's voice more or less trailed off as though she was asking for the impossible and she knew it.

Claire reached out with a smile on her face. "If there is anyone that I know who will make it in her own right, it's you, Fern. You're a proper wolf in sheep's clothing at the moment. Now we need to strip back the sheepskin. Just like Evie had to. If you can make it through the care system, you will make it through anything this world has to offer.

"I've personally never met anyone with such a gritty character and the ability to get something done. And I'm so sorry that I approached the board without asking you. I just thought I was doing the right thing."

As Fern stirred her coffee slowly, the white clouds of cream swirled around, only to disappear completely like the crosswords she had spoken today. She remained quiet and, without taking her eyes of the coffee cup, was reflecting on all that was being said.

"OK!" Fern suddenly stirred as the old self returned in an instant. "I understand what and why you did it. But remember my experience of college is nothing like your experiences of your education. Uncle Maurice wants me to work here and learn from you, Claire. He believes this theatre, and the good people here, are right for me. And in time will teach me a lot of good skills; and that includes respecting others and myself.

"So, I'm really sorry I called you both boujee girls. It was right out of order but you need to remember the people on the schemes have their own views on college education, and how they understand the government's reasoning behind it. The estate people aren't stupid. They know we're locked into the Universal Credit systems or something similarly distasteful to get any money to live on.

"College life for me was just one round of boredom and survival from the crazy boujee girl gang culture, with their knock-offs on show and stupidly long eyelashes. You ask me what I want! Well, I would like to go to university and be the first person in my family to do so. So many people have written me off purely because of my postal code. That's what I would like help with."

Evie gave her an understanding smile before saying, "I totally understand how you feel, Fern. When I was in care, my neighbour, Lizzie, and I had a plan for my future. I had private lessons in English that Lizzie paid for out of her penny income. School was just one problem after another. Especially the number of schools I attended because my foster placement changed so often.

"But me and Lizzie had the plan, and we knew it would be hard work but I passed three A levels. Not top grades but good enough to get me into a university. Please, Fern, believe me, there are other routes to attaining an education and we are here to help you."

Fern interrupted, "But not a local college. It just destroys your will to live."

Both Claire and Evie replied in unison and softly, "No college then."

Claire quickly added, "But you will have to work damned hard at whatever we get arranged. You do understand that, don't you?" Her face tilted to one side as she looked firmly at Fern's face and held her gaze whilst waiting for a response. A smile broke out on the teenager's face for the second time today.

Then at that moment, and what can only be called tears of happiness, trickled down her cheeks.

"Our Fernie girl overwhelmed? Never!" A smiling Claire said.

Over at the counter, Richard could see that the conversation the three women were having was very deep, personal and heavy-going. He kept his distance whilst they continued with their private conversation that was unknown to him, but in fact had by now moved on. The topic had changed to Fern's forthcoming eighteenth birthday party and what she was doing for it.

This led Claire to say in a buoyant voice, "Now we all have our futures to look forward to. But it's going to be a hard slog whatever way you look at it! You two did know that I was adopted at about two years old." This information came like a bolt of lightning from the sky to the young Fern and the not so much older new journalist Evie.

"I thought that would shut you two up!" Adding quietly, "I never told anyone that. So, keep it to yourselves or you two are dead." Claire laughed. "And no, I don't wish to talk about it. All this adoption rubbish you see in documentaries, it's not all it was meant to be. Take it from someone who was adopted."

Evie, Fern and Claire gossiped on as they often did, and it has to be said to the amusement of Richard who never really understood what three intelligent women could possibly find to talk about. If only the three women knew what their destiny held in store for them, they would have plenty to talk about.

The three tough and tenacious hard-hitting workers sat together as sisters in arms. Or more correctly, sisters from care. Comprising of Fern, the procurer; Claire, the planner; and Evie, the wordsmith, deliberating in low voices about their future plans, including the importance of distancing themselves from their own dysfunctional childhoods.

Their perceptive minds and natural cognitive abilities consciously directed them from all notions of becoming victims of the system at all costs. Especially to all the damaging facets that are quietly conditioned in you from a condemnatory childhood spent surrounded by a life of hardships and letdowns. The three spoke truthfully about their childhoods for the first time with each other.

They described how they began life with mothers who constantly put their own needs before her children. Their mothers' incessant partners who would chastise the children in ways not believable by decent folks; their daily lives living on the notorious sink estates.

Alternatively, and for one of the friends, having to deal constantly with over-controlling and over-ambitious adopted parents who did not accept anything but total success, but as they viewed it, and only as they viewed it. Failure was not acceptable, and as Claire put it to the audience, "Evie, you only have to work with Frank. I've had to live with him. And by the way, HER too!" Evie had never heard Claire talk about her family.

All three agreed unanimously that they were not, under any circumstances, going to take on the mantel of the pity me from care syndrome and last, but not least, take on the label of victim or survivor from care. They all agreed that that would be counter mount to giving in into society's blind warp mindset. Meaning that they were to blame in some way for everything that happened to them. Or worse, left feeling dysfunctional in some way.

The women chatted about the various therapies and counselling services thought appropriate for them in care, including sometimes medication and how wrong it all was. Whilst their parents seemed to escape everything that would be considered blame or responsibility. That is until some poor overworked and under-resourced social services departments got involved.

Then the whole world would explode around the child, often ending up being blamed by all and sundry. The joke, if it were funny, that on many occasions other young babies would appear and have to go through the same old madness. These articulated women could not put any real sense or reason behind what had happened to them. Rather putting it down to pure bad moral luck, and this was something they decided to accept, but never condone.

To move forward, they would need all their wits, tenacity and the good fortune of natural beauty about them, if they were to realise their own success in this world. It was their life and no one else's.

To be continued...